# The Kidnapped Bride

## A Patricia Fisher Mystery

## Book 2

Steve Higgs

## Dedication

To Rita Blanche of Canada for providing the name of the criminal overlord,
Dylan O'Donnel

Table of Contents

Leaving Miami

Dinner with the Riffraff

An Offer of Employment

Gangsters

Too Early for Gin?

The Man by the Pool

Inspiration

Murder

Bodypump

Eavesdropping

What Men Want

More Gangsters

Dinner

Dylan O'Donnell, Criminal Overlord

Morning

George

Hostages

Boris the Russian

The Other Woman in my Suite

Begging for Help

A Favour

The Show Must Go On

An Offer They Couldn't Refuse

A Grand Performance

Muffie

Author's note

A FREE Rex and Albert Story

**Free Amber and Buster story**

More Cozy Mystery by Steve Higgs

More Books by Steve Higgs

Free Books and More

**Extract from The Director's Cut**

**Battle on Board**

## Leaving Miami

My pulse was elevated as I rushed back to the car. I hadn't played golf in years, so when new friend Lady Mary Bostihill-Swank suggested a round at the prestigious La Gorce Golf Course, I jumped at the chance. The sun beat down on us from a vivid blue sky and with no one visibly playing behind us, we played in an unhurried fashion, taking out time and nattering.

Consequently, on that glorious Tuesday afternoon, we lost track of the time.

The ship was due to sail at seven o'clock and we were supposed to be back on board by six. It was already after five and the traffic on Collins Avenue was reported to be terrible at this time of day.

Our Purple Cruise Lines appointed driver, Rufus, was waiting at the reception desk of the golf club and quietly arguing with a man in a suit. No doubt Rufus had politely requested that someone find us on the course and in turn politely request that we move our backsides – he would be held partially responsible if we missed the ship.

Rufus sagged with relief when we appeared back in the club's lobby area. Lady Mary and me were sweating from the effort of hurrying in the late afternoon Miami heat, though Lady Mary had been less inclined to increase her pace and much more convinced that the captain wouldn't dare leave without us.

I had reservations about that.

I was quite certain the ship sailed on time.

I might be the guest in the royal suite, but I wasn't actual royalty. 'Sorry. So, so sorry,' I apologised profusely as I approached Rufus. He was already heading for the door.

He remarked, 'I think we might be cutting it a little tight, ladies,' as he held the door for us.

I slipped outside and headed for the luxury town car waiting for us at the kerb. The engine was purring quietly so the interior would be lovely and cool; a refreshing change from the heat of the day which had barely dipped as evening approached.

Lady Mary sauntered out, refusing to look like she was rushing, then waited patiently for Rufus to open her door. I had already gone around to the other side and got in. My seatbelt was on, and I felt real tension that we might miss the ship and have to arrange to catch up with it.

When I expressed my concern earlier, as I tried to hurry Lady Mary in from the eighteenth green, she had simply replied, 'They have a helicopter, darling. If we miss the ship, George will arrange for us to be collected.'

George, her husband, would probably do just that, but it seemed like a lot of unnecessary hassle if we could get back in time instead. I met Lady Mary and her husband George at a captain's table dinner six nights ago when we left Barbados. They had been holidaying there in their summer house and were now heading back to Los Angeles, a place we would dock in two weeks' time, for a book launch. George was a bestselling author and so had not only made a lot of money but could work wherever he wanted when he wasn't involved in promoting whichever book was about to be released.

Over dinner that first night, I commented on her name - Bostihill-Swank - because it was quite unusual and reminded me of the Bostihill animal park I used to visit at a child. That was when I discovered she was the heir to the Bostihill estate and now owned the animal park her grandfather founded. My knowledge of her family's legacy made it a table-wide topic of conversation and we bonded as I drank my first alcohol since the night I came on board.

The decision to drink was one I made consciously two days before the event. I had lost twelve pounds through eating sensibly and starting, then surprisingly sticking to, a regime of exercise that was managed by an on-board personal trainer. It wasn't vanity driving my change in diet and fitness, I was quite happy with who I was, though I will admit that it had been a moment of self-doubt regarding my waistline that had been the catalyst. What had kept it going, was a desire to test myself. I felt stronger from doing more than I thought I could, which combined with solving a three-decade old mystery, was doing wonders for my self-esteem. So, I made peace with my desire to have an occasional drink and on that night selected an old favourite - gin and tonic. It was Lady Mary's favourite too.

Lady Mary was less inclined to resist though, so as the car pulled away from the ornate gardens at the front of the golf club, she opened the cabinet in the back of the town car and started rummaging. 'Gin, dear?' she said, holding up a bottle of Hendrick and two glasses.

'No, thank you, Lady Mary,' I replied. I was too busy staring anxiously out of the window to see that she poured me one anyway. It wasn't until her hand nudged my arm that I saw her holding the glass at arm's length for me to take while she took a healthy gulp of hers.

Reluctantly, but politely, I took the glass and thanked her. 'It will help with your nerves,' she said as she finished hers and reached for the bottle again to make another. 'Honestly, though, I don't know why you worry, darling. Rufus will get us there. Won't you, Rufus?'

Rufus glanced at her via the rear-view mirror as he said, 'I will certainly try, madam.' He was already stuck in traffic though, the narrow strip of land dictating the road was also narrow. The inevitable result was that as people heading home after the daily grind and all converged into one, it ground to a halt.

Lady Mary reached for her bag, fished out her purse and produced several very new looking hundred-dollar bills. She waved them so Rufus could see, his eyes widening slightly at the prize being held aloft. 'Yours if you can get my worrisome friend to the ship in time.'

I didn't like that she could or would show off her money like that, bribing the driver to achieve what he thought was not possible, but I had to admit that her tactic worked. Suddenly, Rufus engaged his local knowledge, turning left through a parking lot and right through the lobby area of a hotel onto a small back road that was barely more than an alleyway. He kept weaving through the street like that until he re-joined the traffic a mile south of where we had been stuck. By then, the road had widened to two lanes and was beginning to pick up speed.

'You see, darling,' said Lady Mary, 'you just have to know where to apply the lever.'

Rufus allowed the car to glide to a halt by the awning that led into the executive area of the ship at twelve minutes after six. The ship's new deputy captain was standing to the left of the awning, his pristine and immaculate white uniform shining in the sun. Beside him were two of the security officers. I was beginning to learn their names, something Lady Mary initially scoffed at until she heard about my period under house arrest.

As the car came to a complete stop, Commander Rutherford, whose first name was Matthew, stepped forward to open the back door for Lady Mary. 'Good evening, Lady Mary,' he said, dipping his head graciously.

Rufus slipped out of his door to open mine and offered me his hand.

'Thank you, Rufus,' I offered with a smile. He had been my chauffer for the last two days while I explored the city, his local knowledge startling until I learned he started his working life as a tour bus guide. 'Thank you for looking after me.'

I air-kissed his cheek as he said, 'You are most welcome, Mrs Fisher.'

'Come along, Patricia,' called Lady Mary as she disappeared inside the ship, her voice echoing back out. 'I can hear sundowners calling.'

I was about to hurry along to catch up when I caught the sound of several cars racing toward me. Turning to see what was happening, I saw three large, black limousines, each with private plates, hurtling in my direction.

Someone was worried they were late.

New arrivals meeting the ship in each location we went to were generally inducted onto the boat much earlier in the day. It allowed for guests to get off after breakfast as they headed off to explore and then return later to find new arrivals already on board. It avoided both parties bumping against one another as they went in opposite directions. If these cars contained new guests, then they were very late to arrive.

Curious or perhaps nosey, I picked a spot next to Lieutenant Richard Stevens, gave him a conspiratorial smile and settled in to watch. He said, 'Good evening, Mrs Fisher,' as he returned my smile. 'How was your visit to Miami?'

'Oh, it was wonderful,' I gushed. 'The architecture is incredible. I had no idea it would be so different. Did you get time to explore?'

'Actually, this is my hometown,' he replied. 'I went to see my mom.'

Any further conversation was cut short by the three limousines screeching to a halt right in front of the awning. Fascinated, I found myself unwilling to move as men in dark suits began emptying from the cars. They were all men, not one woman to break up the demographic, and each had the same or similar short hair style. They were also young, late twenties or early thirties, and every one of them looked fit and capable like they were part of a military team.

The rear doors of the middle car were opened by two of the men who then stepped back to let the people inside out. From the side nearest us emerged a tubby man in his early fifties. He too wore a dark suit, and sunglasses to hide his eyes from the bright light reflecting off the white hull of the ship. His hair, in contrast to his security detail, for that is what I assume they were, was longer and slicked back with a product to keep it in place. He wasn't a handsome man, but he exuded a sense of power and dominance.

From the other side of the car, accepting a hand to get out, was a petite woman in a pretty summer dress. His daughter, no doubt. I watched to see if an older woman would also appear as the wife and mother was missing from the picture, but it turned out the car was now empty.

As the men began unpacking luggage from the car and from a minivan that then pulled up behind the third limousine, I realised that no wife/mother was coming.

Lieutenant Stevens and his partner, whose name I had yet to learn, stepped forward to make official greetings and inspect tickets. He welcomed the new passengers on board and offered to escort them to their suite.

I decided I had been nosey enough and though I didn't want the sundowner drink Lady Mary had most likely already made for me, I did want to get back to my suite. Jermaine would be waiting for me, and I was due to participate in a group spin session my gym instructor friend Barbie was running this evening.

However, as I turned to go, I noticed that the daughter wasn't moving toward the ship and was being beckoned somewhat urgently by her father. She did not look pleased at the prospect of a cruise, her body language displaying both fear and anger. The man nearest her grabbed her right arm just above the elbow and began to frog-march her toward the awning. Weighing half what he did, she was unable to resist but did swipe ineffectually at his hand a few times as she began to spit a torrent of words in Spanish.

Lieutenant Stevens and the other security guard exchanged a quick glance, but the older man stepped up to them at that point saying, 'Sorry, my fiancée is a little upset about leaving Miami. She wants to stay and visit more shops. Honestly, I think she would spend my entire fortune on shoes if she could. You know how women can be.'

His accent was Cuban perhaps, I couldn't tell, but I got the impression English was a second language for him. I was startled to hear the young woman was his fiancée though; there had to be thirty years or more between them.

She was led around the older man, an angry sneer on her face as she offered him a few more choice words. Then, as if remembering something, she really dug her feet in and shouted toward the car, 'Muffie!'

Her call was answered by a bark as a small, long-haired dog bounced out from the back of the car, trailing its lead behind it. The woman yanked herself free to scoop the dog, which leapt happily into her arms. The man who had been forcing her toward the ship, indicated that she should get moving again, which she did, the dog tucked under her chin as she cooed at it.

As she passed me, she paused to make eye contact and I thought she was going to say something. However, as she opened her mouth to speak, she was dragged away again. A fresh string of Spanish curse words filled the air as she was led inside the ship. There, some of the bodyguards were already moving about, operating silently, and waiting for the two men in their white uniforms to show them where they had to go.

No one gave me a second look as the older man and his entire entourage, followed by porters bearing luggage, swept into the ship. There were so many of them, they overwhelmed the capacity of the elevator, forcing me to wait.

I was in no rush though, so I wandered back outside to bask in the Miami sunshine for a while longer. We would set sail within the hour, and I couldn't tell if I would ever be able to return. There was so much of the city I hadn't had the chance to see, but that was true of everywhere we went. I would need multiple around the world trips in order to take it all in.

Leaning against the white railing they set up outside to funnel passengers onto the ship, and with my face turned up to the sun, I was startled when a voice spoke right next to my ear. 'Mrs Fisher.'

I put my hand to my heart and laughed in reaction to the shock. 'Goodness, you scared me,' I said. It was the other security guard, the one whose name I didn't know.

He said, 'I'm terribly sorry, Mrs Fisher,' giving me a professionally apologetic look to go with the words. 'I'm afraid I have to close the ship now. We are sailing in forty minutes and must run through a number of safety checks first.'

I nodded in acknowledgement and said, 'Of course,' as I turned and went into the ship. There was no longer anyone waiting for the elevators, but neither car was available either, so I pushed open the door that led to the stairs as two stewards began bringing in the awning and white fence from outside.

I tried jogging up the stairs, but it was too many decks from where I was to where I needed to go and the bra I had on wasn't designed to hold my chest in place for such activity. I cupped my hands over my boobs to stop them bouncing but after three flights, I was getting out of breath, my arms and legs were starting to ache, and I was perspiring.

To myself I said, 'I guess I need more time on the step machine.' I had pounded out many hours and maybe a million steps since coming on board, but it hadn't resulted in a superhuman ability to beat the need for an elevator.

Accepting defeat after walking up two more flights, my pace getting slower and slower as the burn in my thighs increased, I left the stairwell and waited for the elevator to come. A minute later, just as it pinged its arrival, I heard the ship's giant engine come to life. Most of the time it was barely perceptible, the general hubbub of the ship and the people on it, drowning the noise out, but in the quiet space below decks, the rumble it created was much more noticeable.

Travelling up to the top deck where I was staying in the Windsor Suite, the finest stately rooms on the world's largest and most luxurious cruise liner, my stomach rumbled lightly. My lunch, a light salad with the dressing on the side, had been eaten at half past twelve, earlier than my normal habit but done deliberately so we would have time for the round of golf. Now long forgotten, I needed something else to eat.

Just a couple of weeks ago, I would have reached for the cookies and eaten a handful. Now though, I was challenging myself to give my body more of what it needed and less of what I craved.  Still, I was hungry, and dinner wasn't until eight o'clock.

I tricked my hunger by drinking a pint of water and getting a bath. Of course, I didn't have to run the bath or even turn on the tap to fill my glass of water. No, no. I had a butler to do those things for me and he got quite upset if he found me doing things for myself.

After two weeks, I was beginning to get used to having Jermaine around, but he kept catching me straightening my bed after I got out of it or closing my own curtains because I wanted them closed and I had hands to do it with. Just this morning, he had coughed politely when I finished my breakfast and picked up my plate and coffee cup to take them to the sink. He wanted to be a butler and had worked hard to get to his current position. Since I met him, my needs had become his raison d'être. He rose every morning with the sole intention of making my life simple, stress free and easy. Anything he could do for me, he did.

He lived in a small cabin that was attached to my royal suite and could be accessed via a door in my kitchen. He wore a uniform all day despite the heat, but then he was Jamaican and hadn't seemed particularly bothered by the sweltering temperatures as we sailed through the Caribbean.

I was soaking in the bath thinking about him now. I would get out soon and find my clothes for the evening already laid out for me. He always asked what Madam wanted to wear and ensured it was crisply pressed. My shoes would be buffed and my jewellery polished. He thought of everything and never cut any corners.

The concept still bothered me because I wasn't the kind of person that had a butler. Until I fled my cheating husband and jumped on board this ship, I had been a cleaner. A job I was good at, but not one that was ever going to give me the kind of lifestyle that came with staff. It was, however, the lifestyle I was currently enjoying. The pace of life on board the Aurelia was as hectic or as relaxed as one wanted it to be. Every couple of days, the giant ship arrived somewhere new, and I had never been to any of the places we were scheduled to visit. Each stop meant the opportunity to explore, and while I had come on board alone, I was never alone when I went ashore. There were other singletons aboard, mostly widowed ladies that were a decade or more older than me, but I had also met with married couples, some of which, like Lady Mary, had invited me go ashore with them.

I ate breakfast in my suite each morning, Jermaine serving food from a diet that had been tailored to me by Barbie, the health and fitness expert. While at sea, I took lunch in one of the many wonderful restaurants dotted about the ship and dinner in the exclusive upper deck restaurant where the captain would regularly join his guests. That was where I had met Lady Mary and where I would be eating tonight. Today was a Saturday, which meant the captain hosted and it would be followed by dancing for those that wished to partake.

I wondered where the older man with the future trophy wife was staying. There were a lot of exclusive suites on the top two decks, far too many for me to get to know all of the people staying in them, but I had met a lot of them over dinner during my time on board and would recognise far more than I could name. With their extensive entourage, the Cuban couple would be difficult to house in one suite, but perhaps some of the security hadn't stayed on board or were quartered in cheaper accommodation a few decks further down. Really, what I was wondering, was what impact the new group would have on the general dynamic of the ship. It was peaceful and friendly, with lots of happy couples breezily going about their care-free lives. The new group looked like gangsters; the sort that caused a bar to clear when they went into it.

If they turned up for dinner tonight, I would find out soon enough.

With that thought echoing in my head, I used my toes to pull the plug. Like everything else around me, the bath was the biggest and most sumptuous I had ever been in. The base of it was contoured so that I sat more comfortably, as if it had been specifically moulded to hold my bottom. Jermaine would clean the entire bathroom, or arrange for it to happen, once I had gone to dinner, so when I stepped out, I didn't look back to see if I had left a mess.

Forty minutes later, I was sipping sparkling water that tasted of passionfruit and chatting with the captain. Captain Alistair Huntley, I had learned, was fifty-four years old though he looked at least a decade younger than that. It had been my assumption that he was younger than me, so learning his correct age was a revelation. He was also very good-looking, his tan skin complimenting his brown hair and showing off his white teeth and twinkling blue eyes. There were many admiring glances from the wives of guests, but he seemed oblivious to them all. I knew that he was single but was he married to the sea? Would that term apply?

He was professionally pleasant with everyone, but it felt like more than that with me. Not that I am suggesting any romantic notions, I doubt he would find me attractive, and I have no need of a man at this point in my life; the memory of my cheating husband is still all too present. However, Captain Huntley made for delightful company each time I saw him, and he always made a point of asking me if everything was to my liking. Like this evening, for instance: he had asked my opinion on the restaurant's décor.

'Is it to your liking, Mrs Fisher?' he asked as if my opinion was important to him. That I was the guest in the Windsor Suite, the most prestigious suite on the Aurelia, seemed to carry clout throughout the ship. I couldn't imagine why though. I was still Patricia Fisher, runaway wife and former cleaner. My life had been unspectacular right up until the moment I boarded this vessel and stumbled across a decades old international jewel theft. Due to that event, I had real money that was actually mine for the first time in my life and I was staying on board the ship for free until the end of my three months around the world cruise.

In reply to the captain, I had agreed that the decoration was spectacular, hoping that I was using the word in the right context and not making myself sound extra dumb today. Our conversation was cut short by the arrival of the man and his much younger fiancée. They were preceded by a pair of bodyguards who came into the room with their dark glasses on, looking mean and putting out a threatening vibe which caused people near them to move away. Answering my earlier question about whether all the men I had seen arrive were staying aboard, they continued to file in behind and around the couple as if creating a circle of safety around them at all times.

'Please excuse me, Mrs Fisher,' the captain had said as he left me to greet the new guests.

Their entrance caused a stir in conversation throughout the room, with guests speculating who the couple were. I heard one lady ask if they were royalty from somewhere and another couple discussing if the young woman was a pop star. I didn't think they were either though. I had my own theory forming.

'Ah, there you are, Patricia,' said Lady Mary as she approached from my right. 'I wondered where you had got to.'

'Good evening, Mary,' I replied. Then said, 'Good evening, George,' as her husband arrived, trailing along behind the more gregarious woman as always.

Lady Mary was holding a large balloon glass that had once held a gin and tonic and appeared to have downed a couple already. She stayed remarkably thin considering how much she drank but then I rarely saw her eat. 'Have you seen the latest riffraff to join us?' she asked, seeing my gaze still focused on the new arrivals.

'Do you know who they are?' I asked in reply.

She gave me an odd look. 'Goodness, no, dear. I have not the slightest interest.' It looked like we were going to find out though because the captain was escorting the couple to the large table set out at the far end of the room where the restaurant overlooked the prow of the ship. Their entourage was both following and leading, their eyes not on the couple, but scanning around the room constantly as if looking for danger. At these big Captain's Table events, the room was set out differently than other nights, with tables arranged to seat twelve persons. The captain's table itself seated twenty by invitation only – the invitations meted out to famous, royalty and ordinary alike though Lady Mary had somehow secured seats for herself and George and I for a second Saturday in a row. The event was intended to make guests mingle and converse, many of the senior staff joining the guests to keep the conversation moving.

'Shall we?' I asked, indicating toward the table. I was itching to know more about the new couple. My curious nature taking over again.

'Come along, George,' demanded Lady Mary whose husband had taken interest in a young woman passing through the crowd with a tray of nibbles. His hopeful look vanished as the girl turned away from him, so he trailed along behind his wife again as she strode purposefully toward the captain's table.

As we reached it, the captain turned to greet and introduce us. 'Mr Perez, Miss Gonzalez, I have the pleasure of introducing Lady Mary Bostihill-Swank and George Brown, the noted author, and Mrs Patricia Fisher.' He turned to us. 'This is Eduardo Perez and Cari Gonzalez,' he

15

delivered with a smile. 'They are on their way to Los Angeles to be married.'

'We are doing things a little back to front,' laughed Eduardo as he shook each of our hands. 'We have the honeymoon first on the way to the wedding.'

Where Eduardo was all smiles and contentment, his bride-to-be looked like her smile was forced. She gave our hands a perfunctory shake that was little more than offering it for us to touch. I was watching her now, my curiosity piqued. This should be the happiest time of her life, yet she looked to be distracted by something. She failed to make eye contact with any of us, mostly staring at the floor or her feet as she stood silently in the shadow of her intended.

'Are you expecting trouble or are you paranoid?' asked Lady Mary as she looked at the ring of suits positioned around the room. One quickly learned that she never bothered to beat around the bush and had no interest in preserving other people's feelings.

'Ah, yes,' Eduardo replied with another chuckle. 'Some of my business dealings have attracted unwanted attention from certain parties that might have followed us. I doubt any of my precautions are necessary, but I don't want anything to disturb or disrupt us.'

I turned my attention to Cari. 'How about you, Cari? What are you most looking forward to? We arrive in Rio in a few days.'

Cari mumbled something I didn't hear and made no attempt to make eye contact with anyone. She did try to move away though, which caused a reaction from the two suits nearest her as they moved slightly to form a barrier. She stopped, her unhappy face betraying her anger, but she didn't resist. An awkward silence persisted for a few seconds until thankfully, we were interrupted by the arrival of several more excited couples, each looking almost overwhelmed by their palatial surroundings.

I made good my escape to chat with an English couple that had just arrived, their accents easy to pick out, but I doubted we had seen the end of the drama between Eduardo and Cari.

Hors d'oeuvres were served a few minutes later as a bell was rung, and the wait staff descended on the tables with plate after plate of delicious food. Chance had placed me opposite Cari and Eduardo making it easy for me to observe their behaviour. I was trying to be surreptitious, though I worried I was just staring. Eduardo was having a great time, conversing with those around him and knocking back wine as the staff kept filling it each time it emptied. Cari, in contrast, was almost robotic in her movements. She picked at her food and sipped at her wine but over the course of an hour had not finished a single glass and placed her hand on top of it each time the wait staff came near her with a bottle. She spoke when spoken to and had engaged in small talk with the couple next to her, but they had soon found it to be hard work and moved on to speak with the couple to their other side.

Eduardo was tactile with her, putting his arm around the back of her chair, touching her arm or her leg beneath the table, but the gestures of intimacy were not reciprocated. Nobody else appeared to notice but it was all I could look at now. Combining her behaviour now with what I had seen when they arrived, really made my head itch. More than anything she looked nervous.

As dessert arrived, the unmistakable noise of a helicopter approaching the ship could be heard over the background music of the band playing. Across the table, Eduardo stiffened and looked about. The landing platform was above us but some distance back toward the centre of the ship where it was away from any of the exposed sun decks. He would not be able to see the aircraft unless it came in low, but the colour had drained from his face. Cari leaned toward her fiancé to whisper something to him. It was the first time I had seen her initiate conversation and there was a smile on her face, but whatever she said, it made Eduardo angry, a scowl flitting across his face before he could bring it back under control. Then he waved a hand at her dismissively, summoned two of his bodyguards and carried on eating as she rose from her chair. She dabbed her lips carefully with a napkin and left without another word. The bodyguards followed her out.

The scene was watched by everyone at the table, Eduardo noticing the faces staring at him only once Cari had left. 'She is not feeling well,' he explained weakly, failing to make it sound true.

'Perhaps it's the company,' sniped Lady Mary loud enough for most of the table to hear.

Eduardo didn't react to the comment though. Pretending nothing was amiss, he took a swig of wine and started on his dessert. 'Do helicopters often arrive after the ship sets sail?' he asked, the question clearly aimed at the captain but voiced to the entire table.

It was the captain that answered, 'We have many guests with their own helicopters which they choose to use to come aboard as it is faster than entering below decks. The platform can accommodate two at any time, plus we have our own helicopter stored below the platform which can be raised on hydraulics.' He paused to take a sip of water, but when he put the glass down, he didn't say anything further.

I excused myself to visit the ladies' room just as a woman three along from me, shrieked with laughter at an anecdote George had been regaling his end of the table with. Like many of the guests at the captain's table, she was well lubricated now and George, being a wordsmith, was able to tell a good tale.

Outside the restroom, I found the two dark-suited bodyguards, looking impatient and obviously waiting for Cari Gonzalez to come out. One of them stepped aside as I approached, allowing me to push the door open.

The young woman was the only other person in the room, washing her hands at one of the sinks. Upon seeing me though, she turned and said something in Spanish. I couldn't tell what it was, I had never taken a Spanish lesson in my life, but sensing that I hadn't understood her, she shrugged, patted my arm and left.

When I came out of the restroom the bodyguards and Cari Gonzalez were gone. As I scanned around, wondering what direction they had gone, I noticed, through the portside windows, a helicopter moving away to the west, and I wondered who it was that had arrived. It wasn't unusual for the Aurelia to play host to A list singers; just last week Rod Stewart had crooned at us for an hour. Variety acts such as comedians, and ventriloquists had also featured but my favourite thus far was a magic act, or perhaps the correct term is illusionist that I watched a week ago. He had defied logic with some of the things he had done, culminating in a finale where he teleported across the room. I later discovered that he was never in front of us, but we were looking at a clever image projected onto a piece of glass on the stage.

Just as the helicopter disappeared from sight and I turned to rejoin the guests at dinner, a white uniform of the ship's security passed me, moving at an urgent pace. When I came into the restaurant, he was speaking to the captain his hand cupped to the captain's ear to deliver a whispered message.

As the captain politely excused himself from the table to go with the man, I saw that Eduardo was also leaving, his entourage of bodyguards once again looking about for danger as his entire party left the room. Was this something to do with the unwanted attention Eduardo's business practices had attracted? And why had the captain suddenly left? Something out of the ordinary was happening and it was tweaking my curiosity.

Maybe if I spoke Spanish, I would already know what this was all about. Cari Gonzalez had been trying to tell me something. Perhaps I would find her tomorrow and see if we could manage a conversation with someone to help translate. Of course, as I thought about that and sipped my water, I didn't know that she would be missing by then.

I hadn't stayed late after dinner, and I hadn't had anything alcoholic to drink, so when my butler woke me as instructed, early the following morning, I had a clear head and felt well rested. Don't be fooled into thinking I am suddenly teetotal, I am nothing of the sort, but I am drinking significantly less now than at any point in my adult life and it is because I have discovered the joy of exercise. Perhaps I should say rediscovered, as there was a time in my teens and perhaps early twenties when I was quite fit. Since coming on board though, the belief that my husband had cheated on me because I was no longer young and skinny had led to exercise and that in turn had led to the realisation that I didn't need him and didn't need to be young or skinny to feel attractive and that somehow had freed my mind to enjoy exercise rather than seeing it as punishment for not having a perfect waistline.

My waistline would never be perfect again, but now that I wasn't trying to lose weight, I was losing it anyway.

'Good morning, madam,' Jermaine said, as he neatly pleated the curtains on all eight windows in my bedroom and arranged each one so the exact same amount of glass was showing. 'I trust you slept well.'

I levered myself upright, fighting the bed covers in the enormous, sumptuous bed until I was in a sitting position. Stifling a yawn, I said, 'Good morning, Jermaine. Thank you for asking. I slept peacefully. Is it another fine day outside?'

Jermaine always rose before me, and he went to bed after me; the hours he committed to the job were extraordinary, but I was certain of his contentedness. He had undoubtedly been up an hour already when he woke me at five thirty, his time spent ensuring the royal suite was as immaculate as his uniform. He stood back from the curtains, finally content they were hanging correctly and smiled at me. 'There is nary a cloud in the sky, madam. Miss Berkeley is waiting for you in the living area, madam. Shall I tell her you will be along momentarily?'

As always, Jermaine was giving me the option to send my fitness instructor away should I feel that another hour in bed was more appealing. It was more appealing, but somehow, it also wasn't. I was getting fitter, and I was feeling more confident because of it. There was no good reason to stop other than laziness; I was creating a new version of me.

Less than five minutes later I was wearing new gym gear that I had bought in Miami two days ago when I had spotted a shop, and I was ready to go.

Barbie was waiting for me in my living room, but she wasn't slouched on a couch; no, she was standing on her left foot with her right foot held in her right hand and her left arm out for balance. Her eyes were closed. Yoga was one of the things she was teaching me and let me tell you this about yoga: it's hard. You see people doing yoga and they don't look like they are doing much. At least, not compared with the people on the treadmill or the climber or the ones lifting weights, but it is deceptive. I sweated just as much holding poses in my first yoga session as I did at any other time.

I waited until she opened her eyes. 'Hi, Patty,' she squealed excitedly. Barbie is a size zero, perfectly crafted goddess put on the earth to make all other women feel inadequate. To go with her tiny waist and gravity defying boobs is an utter lack of unnecessary body fat, lustrous blonde hair and a beautiful face. I could hate her if she wasn't so likeable. Stereotyping would have her as a dumb bimbo, but she had a brain and qualifications and probably a plan for her life that she was quietly enacting. I noticed something new though; her eyes were a little puffy as if she had been crying recently. In fact, now that I was looking, the skin under her nose looked a little red like it had been getting blown too many times. Barbie and I were friends in that we had a relationship which extended beyond gym instructor and gym user, but I didn't know much about her really. I didn't even know if she had a boyfriend that she might have broken up with.

It wasn't right for me to ask though, so I replied with, 'Good morning, Barbie,' twisting my waist and bending in place as she had taught me to do before commencing any exercise. 'What are we doing today?'

'Well,' she started, but before she could say anything more, there was a loud knock at my door.

My feet moved as if I was going to answer it but Jermaine's voice saying, 'Madam.' In a warning/pleading tone, stopped them.

Jermaine crossed the floor slowly; butlers never rush, you know. His pace caused the person outside to knock loudly again. The main door to my suite was just off the central living area so I could not see who was at the door, but I recognised the voice; it was the new deputy captain, Matthew Rutherford. He had been promoted into the position when the position became suddenly vacant, but I didn't know if it was a permanent promotion or a temporary one. Curious, I began toward the door, but Jermaine appeared in the doorway to the living area to announce my visitor. He loved the formality of his role. 'Deputy Captain Rutherford begs an audience, madam. Are you available?'

I tried not to sigh at Jermaine's unnecessary pomp and ceremony as I said, 'Yes, yes. Please send him in.'

Jermaine entered the room to allow the deputy captain access then stood to one side in case he might be needed to bring refreshment.

'Should I go?' asked Barbie.

I looked at the man now entering the room when I answered, 'I don't know, Barbie. Let's see what the gentleman wants first, eh?'

The deputy captain had his hat tucked beneath his left arm. He would have doffed it as he came into the suite as all the uniformed staff with hats did, but the first thing I noticed was how tired he looked. Had he been up all night?

He didn't look in a mood to dawdle so I kept quiet to listen to whatever news he had. 'Mrs Fisher, please excuse the intrusion so early in your day. I would have waited but I know you rise early each morning for exercise.'

I interrupted him so he would know I was not upset by his intrusion and would not waste further time on apologies, 'It's fine, Mr Rutherford. Please tell me what has brought you here this morning.'

'Can we sit?' he asked. Instantly, I started to worry. The second highest ranking officer on board the ship needed to speak with me urgently and thought it would be best if I took the news he had sitting down. Barbie appeared at my side suddenly. She sensed that he had grave news too and I wondered who I knew that might have died. Was it Charlie? How would I feel about it if I learned that my estranged husband was dead?

He said, 'Please?' and indicated toward a pair of couches arranged to face one another. As I silently backed into one and sat, he began speaking, 'You were at the captain's table last night, were you not?'

'I was,' I replied, suddenly relieved that this was not the announcement of a dead relative or spouse, but equally curious about where this was going.

'Did you speak much with Mr Perez or Miss Gonzalez?' he asked.

I shook my head. 'I don't think anyone spoke much with Miss Gonzalez. She kept very much to herself all evening.' I didn't feel the need to tell him or anyone else about our one-sided conversation in the ladies' restroom since no message had been passed. 'I didn't speak more than a few words to Mr Perez either. I'm sorry, why is it that you want to know about my conversation with them? Has something happened?'

I had decided to skip the conversation forward, which had caught the man a little off guard. He took a second before speaking again, 'The captain told me to expect you to ask the pertinent questions.' He paused again, then said, 'Miss Gonzalez is missing as are the two men from Mr Perez's security detail that left the restaurant with her. They did not arrive back in their suite and have not been seen since they left the restaurant.'

I thought about that for a second. 'There's more, isn't there?' The deputy captain would be tasked with conducting an investigation and maintaining security on board. His need to ask me about whether I had spoken with the couple or not, would not have driven him to be hammering on my door at this time of the day. There was something else going on.

The man in uniform looked sheepish suddenly. His glowing cheeks contrasting brilliantly with his stark white uniform as he looked at the floor for a moment like a child caught in a lie and being forced to admit the truth. 'Actually, yes there is,' he said. 'Mr Perez is hoping to engage your services to help him find his bride.' I tilted my head to one side slightly thinking I had misheard him. Before I could ask him to repeat himself though, he then said, 'And it would appear that she has been kidnapped.'

Beside me on the couch, Barbie gasped, her hand flying to her mouth as she said, 'Oh, my God!'

'Why do we think she has been kidnapped?' I asked. I had a stack of questions already, but I led with that one because it seemed the most important.

'Because there is a ransom note,' he explained. He looked quite uncomfortable sitting opposite me. His hat was in his hands as he nervously twiddled it.

'Okay, so the lady has been missing for a few hours with her security guards and that would not normally be too much cause for alarm but there is also a ransom note claiming, I assume, that she had been kidnapped. Is that about right?'

'Yes.' He nodded his head vigorously.

I held up a finger to make sure I had his attention. Jermaine took a step closer, enraptured by the mystery being revealed. 'Big question now Mr Rutherford.' I paused to make sure I had his attention. 'Why does Mr Perez want to engage my services and exactly what kind of services does he think I have to offer?'

The deputy captain shrank a little further into the couch. His lips moved a few times as he tried to form a sentence and he fiddled with his hat a little more. Finally, and just before I prompted him, he said, 'I might have told him about the sapphire and how you solved a thirty-year-old case and uncovered a plot by the previous deputy captain to murder several people and make off with the jewel.'

So, there it was. Now I knew why he was in my cabin so early this morning.

'You might have?' I repeated with some derision in my voice. He opened his mouth, but I talked over him, 'I'm not a detective, Mr Rutherford.'

'Neither am I,' he squeaked.

'So... what? You're hoping that I can solve this case?'

To my absolute surprise, the man fell to his knees in front of me and grabbed my hand. 'Please, Mrs Fisher,' he said looking up at me with imploring eyes. 'I don't have the faintest idea what I am doing. The captain expects me to deal with crime on board, but this is way beyond me. I was only promoted into this position because you revealed that Mr Schooner was the one behind the murders. I'll be demoted again in no time if I can't work this out.'

I didn't know what to say. I was just staring at him as I tried to work out what possible reply I could have. I was a cleaner a few weeks ago. I knew nothing about solving crimes or searching for clues other than from what I had learned reading mystery books.

'He is offering a fifty-thousand-dollar reward for anyone that can supply information leading to the return of his fiancée,' he blurted. 'I'm not eligible of course as I am crew, but...'

I was still lost for words; the reward didn't change the fact that I had solved the previous case out of absolute necessity and blind luck. The man supplicating himself at my feet though looked desperate. Telling myself that this would probably play out by itself, and I could just pretend to be helping so Mr Rutherford would feel better, I said, 'Okay.' The deputy captain must have been holding his breath because he almost collapsed when I spoke that single word. I quickly added, 'I can't promise that I will achieve anything though.'

'No, no. Of course not, Mrs Fisher. That would be silly. As long as we are seen to be trying our best.' His relief was obvious. 'When can you start?'

I said, 'Huh?' as I raised an eyebrow.

He had clambered back off of my carpet but was still nervously twiddling his hat and looking at the floor. 'Well, you see... that is to say, well... Mr Perez is... kind of waiting for you.'

'Is he now?' I replied haughtily. I was starting to feel put upon.

Beside me Barbie said, 'We can reschedule for later, Patty.'

'No, I'm not content to jump when asked to,' I replied.

Quietly she said, 'Fifty thousand is a lot of money, Patty.'

Her comment caught me off guard. It was a lot of money. I just didn't believe I was going to see any of it and if there really were kidnappers involved, surely getting myself also involved would be dangerous. I had already said I would though.

Reluctantly, I got to my feet. 'Take me to see Mr Perez then.'

## Gangsters

Barbie and I quickly air kissed as I went out the door with the deputy captain. We agreed that I would find her in the gym after lunch and we would work out what kind of session she could fit into her day. Speed walking to Mr Perez's suite, because Mr Rutherford was in a desperate hurry, I found myself worrying about the missing girl. Cari Gonzalez had the look of someone with a lot on her mind last night. If this was to do with her fiancé's business dealings, had she known they might target her to get back at her husband?

Our journey took us down one deck and from the prow, where my suite was located, to about halfway along the length of the ship. Even at the pace Mr Rutherford was walking, it still took ten minutes to get there. We didn't have to knock on the door though, one of the young men was positioned outside. He still had on his dark suit, sunglasses and communications thing with the curly wire behind his ear. He spoke into his left wrist as we approached, gave a brief but wordless nod to Mr Rutherford and opened the door to allow us entry.

The scene inside was not what I expected. The suite was smaller than mine, of course, because every suite on the ship was smaller than mine. In the case of this particular suite, it meant the door opened directly into the accommodation's living area. Eduardo was sitting imperiously behind a large desk set at the far end of the room to dominate it. His security detail, or whatever you want to call them, were absent with the exception of two men, both of whom were leaning on the desk, looking at something that was spread out to cover the entire surface.

They all looked up as we came in, the two men flanking Eduardo both rising to stand upright again. Whatever they had been discussing was put on hold as the two men fell silent.

Mr Rutherford began speaking before anyone else could, 'Mr Perez, thank you for your patience. This is Mrs Fisher,' he said which drew three sets of eyes to me.

Suddenly in the spotlight of three men who all looked tired and angry, I felt unnerved. What I needed to do was say something pertinent or clever since they somehow expected me to be the answer to their problem. Nothing came to me though, so instead, I waved a hand nervously and said, 'Hi.'

Mr Perez's eyebrows climbed his head as he turned his gaze back to Mr Rutherford. 'This is the woman you told me about?' he asked, his tone incredulous.

Mr Rutherford's mouth opened. He was going to say something, but the comment by Eduardo, his instant dismissal, was the trigger I needed to bring my gumption to the surface. 'Excuse me,' I demanded. 'I have no need to be here. If you have no need for my help, I will let myself out.' With that, I spun on my heel, but Eduardo's voice stopped me.

'I'm sorry, Mrs Fisher,' he said, the timbre of his voice soft for the first time. 'That was rude of me. It has been a... testing night.'

I turned back to face him. His apology made it hard for me to do anything now but agree to help. Any thoughts of explaining that I was just another guest on board the ship died right there. Nevertheless, I felt it was prudent to point out that my ability as a detective had been overplayed. 'Mr Perez, I believe you may have been misled about what I am capable of.'

'There's no need to be modest, Mrs Fisher,' he said. I thought he was going to say more, but he paused to glance at one of his men. The glance meant something to him because he started moving. 'Is there anything else you need?' Eduardo asked, the question aimed at Mr Rutherford.

Mr Rutherford replied with, 'Erm.' He looked confused until Eduardo's man opened the door and waited for him to leave. 'Oh, ah, I'll be going then. Good luck, Mrs Fisher.' He almost ran for the door, his desire to escape all too obvious.

Now though, I was alone with three strange men, and I didn't feel entirely comfortable.

Eduardo spoke first, 'I'm sorry, Mrs Fisher. That man is incompetent. I have been leading him by the hand all night. Can I offer you a drink?'

At least he had manners. 'Water, thank you.' Without instruction, the man still stood by Eduardo's desk went to the kitchen as I walked forward to shake hands. 'Shall we dispense with formalities? I'm Patricia.'

'Eduardo Santiago Sebastian Diego Perez but everyone calls me Mr Perez,' he replied coming around the desk with his right hand extended. His hand was massive compared with mine and meaty like the rest of him. He wanted me to call him Mr Perez; it felt like he was trying to establish a dominant position which irked me, but my nerves prevented me from arguing.

As my hand fell back to my side I tried once again to explain that I was not a detective, 'Mr Perez, as I was saying earlier; my career has nothing to do with solving crimes. Surely, this should be a job for the FBI or some other suitably qualified law enforcement organisation.'

He sat on the front edge of the desk, then thought better and offered to move to the couches. He talked as we crossed the room, 'There are a number of reasons why that cannot happen, Mrs Fisher. The first is that we are in international waters and this ship flies a Bahamian flag so is designated as Bahamian sovereignty. I'm sure you can see how hard it would be to get the Bahamian police involved. There is a more delicate matter at hand though, because my business interests are… shall we say…'

'Illegal?' I asked since he was searching for a suitable word.

'Oh, goodness no,' he replied. 'Everything I do is completely above board.' Mr Perez looked and behaved like he was one of the mob, and if it looks like a duck and quacks like a duck etcetera.

'I understand you have a ransom note,' I said to move things on. At the click of his fingers, one of his men walked over with a plastic Ziplock bag containing a torn off page from a line notepad. He handed it to Mr Perez, who handed it to me.

On the note was three words: I warned you.

It was cryptic to say the least.

There was no imperative driving me to investigate the whereabouts of the missing woman, but… I was interested. Life on board the Aurelia was wonderful, but something exciting to do might be nice too. 'Will you help me find my Cari?' he asked, his voice hushed as if nervous I might say no. Weighing things up, not only did I not feel like I could say no, but I also felt like I might be the right person to unravel her whereabouts. She had to be on the ship, and I had just solved a far more difficult case after all. I was still holding the ransom note in my hands, the three words on it defying explanation for now. I settled into a comfortable position on the chair and handed the note back to Mr Perez. Then I rooted around in my handbag to produce a notebook and pen.

Over the next hour I learned all that Mr Perez wanted to tell me. I phrase it like that deliberately because I have no doubt he was withholding information. For instance, he assured me that he and Cari were very much in love. I made no comment, but his claim failed to align

32

with what I had seen. The happy couple were on their way to Los Angeles, a twenty-seven-day passage during which the Aurelia would stop several times. There they would be married in a private ceremony, and they were relocating their business there after some *problems* in Miami that he did not wish to expand on because, he assured me, they were not pertinent to the case.

When he finished telling me what he thought I needed to know, I asked, 'Who arrived by helicopter last night?'

'I don't know,' he replied. 'I did not see them.'

'But you suspect that you know and that is why you left dinner prematurely, right?'

He sighed. 'Mrs Fisher, I suspect that one or more groups of what you might refer to as organised crime families came aboard last night looking for me. One of them has Cari and they will use her to get to me.'

'Why?' I asked.

Mr Perez leaned back in his chair and thought for a second before answering. 'Because I am a legitimate businessman that got caught up in their affairs. I own a successful club in Miami which they wanted and when I refused to sell it to them, they tried to squeeze me out. They blockaded my liquor so I couldn't buy any, but I found new suppliers. They scared off my staff, but I found new people to employ. They refused to take no for an answer and demanded I hand over the deeds to the property under threat of death. So, I sold the business to them but set fire to it as I left. I knew it would cause trouble, but I just couldn't help myself. We escaped to the ship with a plan to start a new life on the other side of the country. I thought we had escaped them until the helicopter arrived. Now my Cari is missing, and I don't know what they might do to her if I don't give myself up. There's been no contact yet though so I couldn't do that, even if I wanted to.'

'Who could it be?' I asked. 'Which crime families?' I didn't have any idea what I was going to do with the information I was gathering, but it sounded like the right question to ask.

He thought about it for a few seconds before he replied, 'The Caprione family might.'

This prompted the man to his left to voice his opinion. The two guards had come to stand behind the couch Mr Perez was sitting on, standing silently like two sentinels. This was the first time I had heard any of them speak. 'Nah, boss, they would never be so bold. It's more likely to be the Polish.'

This caused the third man to chip in, 'Or the Russians. You can never be sure what the crazy Russians will do.'

'Yeah, it could be Boris's men,' replied henchman number one.

'Boris?' questioned Mr Perez. 'He is a personal friend. He's coming to the wedding.'

'Yeah but, he was awful sore about you taking that shipment from him last year. You had to kill six of his men if you remember.' Henchman number one had said too much, his cheeks colouring from the look his boss gave him. If Mr Perez thought he was convincing me or anyone else that he was a legitimate businessman, then he was fooling himself. He growled something quietly in Spanish that I didn't understand, the henchman fell silent and looked shamefacedly at the carpet.

Finally, he turned his face back to mine. 'Sorry about that, Mrs Fisher. Some of my men have over-active imaginations,' he lied.

'What I am hearing is that you have a number of enemies and any one of them might have taken Cari in retribution for destroying the club you sold them. The ransom note: *I warned you.* It seems like the person writing it believes the person reading it will know what they are referring to.'

Mr Perez nodded. 'It does look like that. I wish I could tell you more. Maybe it is a mistake, but it doesn't mean anything to me.'

I pursed my lips as I questioned whether I should challenge him on what he was telling me. Common sense prevailed though since I doubted it was a good idea to call a gangster a liar in his own cabin while he is flanked by his bodyguards. Instead, I said, 'Tell me about the two men that went missing with Cari last night.'

## Too Early for Gin?

It was almost another thirty minutes before I felt I had exhausted my questions. Had I felt he was telling me the whole truth I might have had more questions for him, but since he was being economic with the facts, presumably because he didn't want to incriminate himself, I figured I would be better off seeking out Mr Rutherford; I could ask him who had arrived by helicopter and see if the names matched any that Eduardo Perez had provided.

Before I went looking for him, I needed some breakfast, but on my way back to my suite, I bumped into Lady Mary. As usual she was without her husband, I rarely saw them doing things together, perhaps that was their secret to a happy marriage, and, as usual, she had a drink in her hand.

'Patricia, darling,' she drawled when she spotted me. 'I missed saying goodnight to you last night. When I looked for you, you had already departed, naughty girl.' As she gently chastised me, she sank the rest of the buck's fizz she was holding and found a nearby flowerpot to leave the glass in.

I didn't bother pointing out that I had received a slightly drunken hug goodnight from her as I left the restaurant last night, she would instantly deny having been too squiffy to remember. It was one of her charms that she knew she was a bit of a lush but was too posh for the term to apply. Instead, she was a socialite because that was far more respectable.

Now that her hands were empty, she took a compact from her handbag to check her face and moved to a window a few feet away that looked out over the top deck sun terrace. As she gazed out, she said, 'Where are you going anyway, sweetie, you look like you are dressed for another of your crazy exercise sessions? I thought you might like to conspire by the pool until the hour was decent enough for cocktails.'

'Didn't you just have a cocktail?' I asked, knowing full well that she had.

She tutted in response, 'That was just breakfast, sweetie. It hardly counts. I did hear a little snippet of gossip though.' Lady Mary dropped her voice and leaned in to whisper, 'The couple at the table behind me were saying that a young woman has gone missing. Those goons from last night, the ones in dark suits that never spoke or smiled, were chasing all over the ship looking for her. Do you suppose it was that poor girl that was with that awful man at dinner? You know, the one that thinks he's some kind of mafia boss?'

'I couldn't possibly say.' I replied trying to sound innocent.

Lady Mary wasn't fooled though. 'You know something, don't you, Patricia?' When I didn't answer and she could see I was trying to work out what I could say, she said, 'Do spill, darling. I simply must know. There's all too little excitement on this ship.'

I opened my mouth to say something that would deflect her, but I already knew she would just keep pestering me until I told her everything. Instead, I figured I could just give her the buzz she was after. I looked about in a deliberate show of making sure no one was watching us or within earshot, then said, 'Not here,' at a bare whisper. With a quick incline of my head, I had her follow me back to my suite.

Jermaine appeared within seconds as always. 'Madam,' he acknowledged. 'And Lady Mary, good morning. May I offer you refreshments?' He was standing just inside the living area as we went in. As always, he looked tall and capable, his hands clasped behind his back as if he were on parade.

I looked at Lady Mary to gauge her opinion. 'Too early for gin?' she asked.

'Much too early,' I replied, just about keeping my eye roll in check. 'Can you prepare some breakfast please, Jermaine? And iced tea for two.'

He said, 'Very good, madam.' Then he bustled away to the kitchen as I guided Lady Mary to the suite's private sun terrace.

'Oh, this is lovely, Patricia,' gushed Lady Mary as she came through the sliding doors and into the sun. 'I had no idea your suite had its own terrace. Oh, this is so much better than hanging out by the pool. Do you know, there were children there last week?'

'Were they noisy? I asked. I hadn't heard a child at any point during my time aboard.

'Goodness, no. They were just there. That's bad enough. Now don't try changing the subject, Patricia sweetie. Tell me what you know about the mafia boss and his missing bride.'

I settled onto a sun-lounger and fixed Lady Mary with a focused gaze. 'The girl isn't just missing. She was kidnapped,' I said, delivering the news like a hammy actor on an old TV show. It made Lady Mary gasp though. 'There is a ransom note and Eduardo wants me to help him find her.'

Lady Mary took her hand from her mouth in confusion. 'Who is Eduardo?'

'That's your mafia boss,' I replied. Lady Mary had been introduced to them at the same time as me but had most likely not even bothered to register their names. 'His name is Eduardo Perez, and the missing girl is called Cari Gonzalez. The two bodyguards that left with her are also missing.'

The confused look on Lady Mary's face was deepening though. 'How do you know all this and why would he come to you for help?' she asked.

I had accepted that I would have to tell her a few things about my recent past when I started talking. I got a few more moments respite though as Jermaine arrived with a pitcher of iced tea, made fresh not from a carton, and two glasses with slices of freshly cut lemon. He served in silence and withdrew again.

I took a sip of my drink and started talking again, 'Did you hear anything about a stolen sapphire being found just before you came on board in Barbados?'

Lady Mary had sipped at her drink as well but placed it back on the small table by her lounger as she replied, 'Yes I did. Quite the scandal I heard. The deputy captain jumped overboard and there was a murder and a chase around the ship.' She leaned forward as if she were about to share a big secret. 'I heard the whole case was solved by a woman that had come on board by hersel...' Lady Mary's voice trailed off as realisation dawned. Then she said, 'No! Patricia. It was you?'

I felt my cheeks flush with a little bit of embarrassment, but I nodded. 'It was mostly accident and necessity, but yes, it was me, and because of it, the new deputy captain, Mr Rutherford, volunteered my detective services to Mr Perez.' I was boasting but I had kept my secret for a week since I had met her, and I was desperate to bask in someone's admiration.

'We'll circle back to Mr Perez, darling. I need to hear about the sapphire. Was it really as big as a man's fist?'

'Bigger,' I replied. Then, because I knew there was no way out of it, and because secretly I was bursting to tell people, I regaled Lady Mary with the whole story, all the way back to catching Charlie with my best friend.

Jermaine served my breakfast while I talked and endured me telling Lady Mary about his part in my adventure. Lady Mary provided gasps and a few other noises to indicate wonder or appreciation and at the end, when I told her about the sapphire, she clapped.

'So, anyway,' I continued, 'Eduardo now thinks I am some kind of sleuth, and he wants me to investigate on his behalf. The authorities cannot easily get involved and I don't think he wants them to.'

'Why ever not?' she interrupted.

'Because I think he might actually be a mafia boss. He certainly gives the impression that he is or has been involved in some shady dealings and there are people that might want to hurt him.'

'You think someone took Miss Gonzalez to get to him?' Lady Mary asked.

'That's one theory,' I acknowledged. 'I'm not sure I want to draw any conclusions yet though.'

Lady Mary nodded knowingly. 'Of course. Everyone could be a suspect.'

'That would make a lot of suspects. We have three days until we make port again though, so I think I will poke around and see what I can turn up.'

Suddenly Lady Mary sprang to her feet and grabbed her head with both hands. She looked like she had just remembered she left the bath running in her house or something. 'Oh, my God. Oh, my God. Oh, my God. I just remembered.'

'What?' I demanded; drawn to know what it was that had shocked her.

She paced to the edge of the terrace and turned around to face me, a look of horror on her face. 'I think I know who the kidnapper is!' she exclaimed breathlessly.

'I'll know him if I see him again,' Lady Mary assured me. It wasn't very assuring though. My titled friend was convinced she had overheard a man plotting kidnap and murder by the pool three days ago, just as we were sailing into Miami. According to her, the man had been on a sun-lounger within earshot as she worked on her tan and George hid beneath an umbrella to spare his milky white skin while he worked on his next thriller. She hadn't paid much attention at the time, but the man had been running through different ways to kill a person and had been doing so out loud.

It sounded ridiculous, but she was adamant. He was still there when she left to get changed for going ashore, looking in his direction only once as she stood up to leave. 'I remember his face because I saw it again later that night as we came back to the ship. He was hanging around near the main entrance. I think... he looked like he wanted to speak with me, like maybe he realised I had overheard him plotting and wanted to lie to me and tell me it wasn't what I thought. He didn't come over though and when I asked George what he thought, he said he hadn't even noticed. Well, you know what George is like, living in that dream world of his.'

We were on the upper deck sun terrace looking for the man now. Not that I was looking because Lady Mary hadn't been able to supply anything useful to describe him. When I had prompted her with questions like whether he was tall or short, fat or thin, she had said average to all of them. 'He had hair,' was her answer to my question about his hair style and colour. The best she could commit to was maybe red or brown.

'I'll know him if I see him again,' she said for perhaps the fifth time. We had completed three laps of the terrace though and she hadn't seen anyone that she thought was the man she wanted. I couldn't tell if this was a wild goose chase or not, but it was beginning to feel like one.

Rather than express that and show that I doubted her, I said, 'Perhaps we should sit in the sun for a while and see if he shows. What do you think?'

Lady Mary checked her watch then glanced at the pool bar. 'I am getting thirsty,' she said. 'Maybe we should get a drink and cool off, yes?' I chuckled to myself as I nodded. A drink sounded good, but my choice of beverage would be different to what Lady Mary had in mind. As we slid onto two stools in the shade on the open bar, my friend held up her hand to get the barman's attention, then ordered two cosmopolitans.

'Not for me, I'll have water, thanks.' I butted in quickly.

Lady Mary slid her sunglasses down her nose so she could peer over the top of them at me. 'The two cosmos are for me, darling.'

The tall Scandinavian-looking barman was a hunk full of muscle. I could see Lady Mary eyeing him up as he shook up her cocktails, his muscular biceps poking out from the cuff of his polo shirt. He handed over the cocktails, opened a litre bottle of sparkling water for me and said, 'Thank you, ladies,' as he swiped Lady Mary's card.

'He could make me forget I was married,' muttered Lady Mary just loud enough for him to hear once we had turned around to scan the terrace again.

'Lady Mary!' I chastised her. 'You wouldn't.'

'No, dear, of course not. Wouldn't dream of it,' she replied in a tone that suggested she might climb him like a cat up a tree given the chance. He had to be twenty years younger than either one of us.

For the next thirty minutes, I drank my water while Lady Mary finished her cosmos and ordered two more. She didn't spot anyone that looked like the man she continually stated she would recognise so at twelve noon I called time on the pool-side stakeout. I didn't want to waste the whole day doing nothing and my bum was going to sleep on the bar stool.

'What do we do now then?' Lady Mary asked as she stifled a yawn.

'I think I will track down my fitness instructor and reorganise the session I missed this morning.' Lady Mary looked sickened by the idea.

'What is with all the fitness you persist in doing, sweetie?' Lady Mary asked. 'It can't be good for you.'

I gave her an honest reply. 'Actually, it's a new thing but I feel pretty good since I started doing it. I started a couple of weeks ago, but what was difficult then, is my warm-up now. I feel stronger and fitter and more capable. You should try it.' I hadn't meant to say the last sentence, forcing my preferences onto others was not a habit I would promote, but the words were out now, and Lady Mary was considering them.

'You feel stronger and more capable, eh? Are you going there now?' she asked.

'I want to rearrange a session I missed this morning but then I have to find Mr Rutherford.' I didn't add that I had planned to find Mr Rutherford hours ago but had been distracted by Lady Mary's search for a mystery killer by the pool.

'I think I will come with you, Patricia dear. Maybe I will watch and see what all the fuss is with this fitness malarkey.' Inadvertently I had swayed her course. Had I not, she probably would have gone back to her suite for a lie down.

On the way from the upper deck sun terrace to the exclusive upper deck gym, my stomach gave a light rumble to remind me that my breakfast of scrambled eggs and smoked salmon wasn't sufficient, in its opinion, to sustain me. I would find Barbie first though and see when she could fit me in. Lady Mary and I found her in the gym, which wasn't much of a shock. As I went to the counter to speak with her, Lady Mary wandered across to the doors to look into the gym. The first thing I noticed was that Barbie's eyes looked even more puffy than this morning. 'Is everything alright?' I asked.

She raised her eyebrows, surprised by the question. 'Yes, I just got off the phone with Mr Rutherford two seconds ago. He called here trying to find you.'

'Oh. Did he say what he wanted?'

'Not really,' she replied picking up the phone again. 'He asked me to call him if you showed up here and to tell you that he had information pertinent to your investigation. Patty, are you involved in something again?'

She was poised with her finger over the buttons to make the call to Mr Rutherford and was watching my face as I tried to work out what it wanted to do. I was wrestling with a natural inclination to give her a rueful smile and the belief that I needed to be more serious. I settled for a shrug and a lopsided grin.

'I'm taking that for a yes, Patty. Do I call him?' I nodded, at which she glanced down to see what her hand was doing. A second passed while she waited for it to connect. 'Mr Rutherford? Mrs Fisher just arrived.' I heard the muffled sound of a man's voice at the other end but could not make out what he was saying. She said, 'Uh-huh.' In response to something. 'Uh-huh.' Again. Then, 'On deck five in the laundry room next to elevator bank four. I understand.' She replaced the phone on the desk.

'What did he find?' I asked.

'Oh,' she replied as if surprised by my question. 'I didn't ask him that. He asked that I bring you to where he is, if that was convenient for you.' She was already gathering her things to leave.

I pursed my lips. 'Did he make it sound like he was expecting me along shortly? I was hoping you might like some lunch and we could rearrange my morning workout.' After my less than amusing time with Mr Schooner, the former deputy captain, I was disinclined to have this one make demands of me.

'No,' she said after a moment. 'Mostly he sounded desperate, like he did this morning in your suite.' Barbie slid her phone into a slot in the fabric on her skin-tight lycra leggings just by her right hip but paused at my question to consider it. She put a hand to her perfectly flat belly, which today was exposed to show her tight, lean abdominal muscles, then said, 'I do need to eat. There's a really nice place that serves incredible vegan pastries we could visit on the way back.

'Vegan pastries?' Lady Mary had her top lip curled in a show of disgust.

'Hello,' said Barbie, taking in my companion for the first time. 'I'm Barbie. Welcome to the top deck gym. Will you be taking a class with us while you are on board? Patricia started just a few weeks ago and she has been such an inspiration to us all.'

*An inspiration.* I swelled with pride, then realised she had done it again. Barbie was always finding subtle ways to motivate people. Lady Mary had been suckered in too though and was now looking through the

46

window into the gym again. 'There are some rather nice-looking men in there. Do we get to pick our instructor?'

'Um, possibly,' replied Barbie, a little thrown by the question.

'I might be swayed to give it a go if this one is available,' said Lady Mary as she pointed through the window. 'Here he comes now in fact.'

Lady Mary took a step back to allow the man to come through the door. He offered her a polite smile, then said, 'What?' because the three women in the gym reception were all staring at him wordlessly. He was one of Barbie's fellow instructors and quite the hunk of man. Much like Barbie, his gym vest looked to be sprayed directly onto his torso which was utterly devoid of fat. A touch of grey around his temples suggested his age was somewhere close to forty but his face was free of wrinkles, and he was quite good-looking with a strong jaw bearing a three-day stubble. His ebony skin glistened with a light sheen of sweat from whatever he had been doing.

'Mark, this is Lady Mary, she is considering taking some classes with us.' Barbie wisely brushed over the part where Lady Mary wanted to cover him in toffee sauce and eat him with a spoon. She was currently eyeing up his muscular bum but averted her eyes as he turned to face her.

'We can certainly help you out with whatever goals you might have. Strength and conditioning, body sculpting, general fitness... perhaps we can make an appointment for you to return and discuss goals.'

'Perhaps,' Lady Mary replied which surprised me because this didn't seem like her thing at all.

While she chatted with Mark, I brought Barbie's attention back to me. 'Before we find Mr Rutherford,' I had decided to go to him since I wanted to ask him about the helicopters, 'can we rearrange my one to one. When are you free later?'

'Great idea,' she beamed at me, then slid back behind the counter to open a screen on the computer. 'I have an opening at...'

'What's that class?' I asked, pointing at the screen to an hour block labelled bodypump. Beneath the name of the class was her name to show that she was instructing.

'Bodypump?' she confirmed. 'That's a great class, Patty. It's a little, um...'

'What?'

'Well, it's one of our advanced classes.' Her voice was guarded, clearly not saying something.'

'You don't think I can do it?'

'Goodness, no, Patty. You can absolutely give it a go, if you want to.'

'Give what a go?' asked Lady Mary. Mark had gone back into the gym.

'A bodypump class,' I replied. 'It's on at two o'clock.' Glancing at the clock, I calculated that there ought to be plenty of time for lunch and to visit Mr Rutherford wherever he was.

'Perhaps I should watch the class before I commit to do anything else,' she suggested.

Thinking that I could inspire her, I said, 'Great idea.' I noticed that Barbie didn't look so sure though.

'Well, I'll see you back here at two then. I have no interest in vegan pastries, so I shall leave you to seek out Mr Rutherford, sweetie.' She

48

leaned in for a quick air-kiss and left me with Barbie as she went in search of her own lunch, one that would probably have a liquid content.

Next to me, Barbie was stretching her long arms above her head. She then bent at the waist to press her forehead to her shins, stood up and asked, 'Ready?'

'Ready for what?'

'I thought we could jog and take the stairs rather than using the elevators,' she suggested like it was a great idea. 'We can work up an appetite for lunch because, after all, vegan pastries are still pastries.'

'Um, okay,' I mumbled, a little surprised that I was now going for a run with a woman that looked like she was genetically closer to a gazelle than she was to me. 'How far away is he?'

'Deck five.'

My eyes widened. 'Deck five? How many flights of stairs is that?' We were on deck twenty, so it was a lot, and the ship is half a kilometre long.

'Challenge time, Patty. Let's push ourselves! There's nothing like taking the workout outside the gym to really target our plateaus.' There was no fighting it, Barbie was all fired up and excited now. Her personality was what most people would call effervescent. Other's might call it annoying, of course, but she was perpetually in a positive mood and had already started jogging on the spot.

'I have a bag,' I pointed out in the faint hope that she would change her mind. Instead, she produced a small backpack from behind the counter and helped me zip my bag into it. Now that it was secured on my back, we set off to find Mr Rutherford.

Twenty minutes later, we arrived at the laundry room to find one of the ship's security detail in his pristine white uniform waiting outside of the door. He smiled as we approached, his eyes very much on Barbie and not me though. I was sweating like a pig, my hair hanging in clumps where my perspiration had got to it and flying in frizzy curls where it had not. Barbie had to have some kind of special deal with the devil though. Not only did she look perfect, have a beautiful face and flawless body, but where I had enormous armpit stains of sweat, all she had was a few beads of it finally forming on her brow.

'Hi, Glen,' she said as we slowed to a walk for the last few metres. I was just thankful we had stopped and that she had let me go at a pace that didn't mean I was now hugging the wall and gasping for breath. Barbie clearly knew the man, though he wasn't one that I recognised. 'Is Mr Rutherford inside?' Barbie asked.

'Yes.' He looked at me finally, his smile slipping as he took in the sweat monster from the black lagoon. 'Mrs Fisher, yes.' I nodded and managed a weak thumbs up because I was still out of breath. 'Mr Rutherford is waiting for you inside. Barbie you might want to stay out here and keep me company. It's not nice in there; unless you like dead bodies.'

'There's a body in there?' Barbie and I both said at the same time.

Just then the door opened from the inside and Mr Rutherford stuck his head out. He looked more exhausted than the last time I had seen him, and his uniform was more rumpled yet. He also looked stressed. 'Mrs Fisher. Thank you for coming. We found one of the bodyguards that left the restaurant with Miss Gonzalez last night. He's been shot.'

He inclined his head back inside the room, so I followed him, leaving Barbie outside to chat with Glen. She didn't need to see this any more than I wanted to. Until two weeks ago, I had never seen a dead body, apart from my grandfather when he had an open-casket funeral, that is. This would be my third since coming on board the Aurelia two weeks ago.

Inside, the room was vast. Ten times the size of my suite and filled with machinery that ought to be making gurgling washing noises but was strangely silent. There were pipes running along the ceiling and down into huge industrial washing machines which were arranged in banks. Laundry bags, both full and empty ones were stacked in mostly neat piles all over the place. There were no staff in sight although the room was clearly designed to be filled with them. Mr Rutherford explained as he led me through the room and around a bulkhead, 'The cleaners send bags down chutes throughout the ship to arrive in a series of laundry rooms. There is a lot of bed linen and towels to be cleaned every day. Guest clothes are dealt with in a different way of course, but this is one of six laundry rooms dealing with the daily demand for fresh tablecloths, towels by the pool, etcetera. An hour ago, one of the crew found a laundry bag that was too heavy to be filled with towels.' As he said that we rounded a corner which brought us to the exit from the laundry chute. There were five men in the space, all of them doing nothing and not talking. Three of them were Mr Rutherford's ship security team, the remaining two wore dark suits and were clearly Eduardo's men.

On the deck between them was a sixth man, his feet and lower legs still in a laundry bag. There was a hole in his forehead.

'It looks like an execution,' said Mr Rutherford. I had to wonder what experience he was basing his opinion on, but I also had to agree that a single shot to the forehead, for there were no other visible wounds I could see, did look like he had been executed.

51

Earlier today, Eduardo had told me the names of the two bodyguards that had left with Cari last night. Mentally referring to my notes, they were Hugo Montoya and Enrique Garcia. The man with the hole in his head had to be Hugo Montoya because I knew Enrique to be in his mid-twenties and this man clearly wasn't.

I confirmed my thoughts anyway. 'This is Hugo?' I asked, looking at Eduardo's guards.

'Yes,' the one on the left replied.

'Any sign of Enrique?'

He shook his head. Turning my head toward Mr Rutherford, I asked, 'Have you been able to establish where he came into the laundry system? I assume there is more than one entry point to the chute.'

He looked panicked for a second, like a rabbit caught in headlights he was unable to move. Everyone was looking at him, he gulped. 'I hadn't thought of that,' he admitted.

'Oh,' I responded instinctively, a little taken aback. 'Oh, well, you should do it now then.' How had he missed the need to find out where the body had been stuffed into the laundry chute? Someone had shot him, then put him into the laundry bag and then stuffed him into the chute. 'There has to be some blood somewhere. It might not tell us where Cari Gonzalez was, but it will be a good starting place.'

When he flapped his lips a few times and nothing came out, I took his arm and walked him around the corner. A better term might be frog-marched, but I tried to resist dragging him and he was wise enough to not resist.

'Mr Rutherford,' I said once we were out of earshot. 'You have to pull yourself together. This really isn't that difficult. Get your men to move the body to the medical centre where I know they have a cold store just in case they ever have a guest drop dead. Then get some more men to start looking at all the access points to the laundry system. When they work out where Hugo was pushed in, they will have narrowed down which deck he was killed on.' He was listening to all I was saying but it didn't look like much of it was taking root. 'Try to think of it as a big jigsaw puzzle. We need to find the edges before we can fill in the middle. At the moment, we don't know what the picture is, but we keep putting pieces together until we do.'

He dropped his head, but he nodded. Then raised it again and said, 'Thank you, Mrs Fisher. Sorry, I am feeling a bit overwhelmed. I'll organise the men and I'll let you know what they discover.' He left me to go back to the body and the men waiting there so I followed him, listened to him give orders to his lieutenants and begin speaking into his radio to direct the effort of unseen others. He appeared to have found surer footing for now.

'Mr Perez will want to see you,' said one of his goons as he took a step toward me. His colleague moved as well so the two men were suddenly crowding me.

I looked up at their emotionless faces. 'Then it's a good thing I want to see him, isn't it?' I replied, making myself sound far more confident than I was feeling. Eduardo Perez and his men were scary people; the kind you read about in books where their enemies end up in the landfill. I didn't move though, and the two men continued to loom over me.

'We will escort you,' said the one that had previously spoken.

I had no intention of being led around and told where I could go. 'Thank you, but no. I'll be along shortly,' I replied.

He was not put off though. 'It would be better if you came with us,' he replied, this time reaching for my arm.

It was slapped away by Mr Rutherford. 'I say, old boy,' he said. 'No touching the guests.'

The man's eyes were like daggers as he looked down at Mr Rutherford but beyond that he didn't react other than to say, 'Very good, Mrs Fisher.' He was staring at Mr Rutherford when he said it, giving me a sense that there might be trouble to come. Then he pushed between us, the other man on his heel as they left.

I blew out a silent sigh of relief. 'They're rather intense chaps, aren't they?' observed Mr Rutherford. 'Should I assign a detail to assist you?'

I considered reminding him that it was his fault I was involved in the first place. I resisted though, instead reinforcing his need to move the body and trace where the man had been killed. Then I remembered the helicopter I wanted to ask him about.

'Ah,' he said. 'I'm not sure how much I can tell you, Mrs Fisher. It is quite sensitive information.'

'Does it pertain to the missing girl?' I asked, now really curious. 'Who are our mystery guests?'

Mr Rutherford leaned against a handy workbench looking tired. 'That's just it, Mrs Fisher. They are a mystery.'

'How so?'

'The helicopter pad isn't manned full time but falls under the remit of the security team to react when a helicopter lands. Normally, we get notice; the pilot requesting permission to use the helipad. Yesterday, the aircraft was upon us before we realised it intended to land and whoever was on board was on the ship before our security could get there. Two of my guards were close enough to intercept them as they joined the top deck, but they were set upon and overpowered by superior numbers. I have men looking for them now.'

'It's a big ship though,' I said, acknowledging the difficulty of the task. 'So, there are some people on board that are now stowaways and they have already demonstrated a willingness to do violence?'

'Mrs Fisher, you cannot tell anyone of this,' he pleaded. 'The captain will have my head if the guests find out.'

'What is he going to do?'

'He expects me to find them. Ship security is my primary task. They didn't use weapons to get on board, so we are hoping that they are not armed. Of course, the rather dead gentleman in the laundry bag would suggest otherwise.'

Yes, he did. I left Mr Rutherford to worry about uninvited guests as I went back out into the passage where Barbie was still waiting. I found her still chatting with the man standing guard outside the door.

'Ready to go?' she asked. 'Vegan pastries await.'

I was a soggy mess and needed a shower, but I was also hungry, so I followed her to the vegan pastry place, carbing up as instructed because she said I would need energy to burn for the bodypump class. It was more than an hour away, yet which gave us time to chat as we drank our water.

'Is everything alright, Barbie?' I asked.

She had a curious look on her face when she looked back at me. 'You asked me that earlier too, Patty. Why the concern?'

'Your eyes look puffy, like you are upset about something and have been crying,' I replied going to the honest approach.

She chuckled. 'It's nothing like that, Patty. I don't know what it is. They itch and I have been sneezing. Almost as if I have hay fever this far out on the ocean.'

'That's all?' I confirmed, wanting to see if there might be something else bothering her and hoping we were close enough friends for her to feel she could tell me.

'That's all. Nothing exciting to tell you, I'm afraid.' She checked the time on her phone. 'I should be heading back. I need to set up for the class. Are you sure you still want to try it?' she said as if trying to put me off. Which was strange because all she ever did was push me and encourage me and get me to do more than I thought I could.

I wasn't being put off though. I was ready for this. I was inspirational!

## Bodypump

'Cooee, Patricia sweetie,' called Lady Mary. I had just reached the outer door to the gym and was about to go inside when she called me. She was sauntering along the passage toward me, the sun shining through the windows to light her up. She had on brand new sports gear that looked shop fresh.

'I thought you were planning to watch,' I said, curious about her outfit.

'Goodness, yes, Patricia darling. One has to look the part though, even for spectating. I'm not convinced all this exercise is good for a person. Besides, I'm not really a fan of perspiring. I'd rather stay thin by not eating.'

I wasn't a fan of perspiring either, especially since I was so good at it. I had showered and changed into fresh sports gear after the *gentle* jog Barbie and I took earlier, and I was feeling ready for my bodypump class. Actually, I was telling myself I was ready while feeling quite trepidatious.

There were other people in the gym, putting their bottles of water to one side and stretching off as Lady Mary and I made our way into the exercise area set off to one side in front of a wall of mirrors.

Lady Mary was looking around in fascination like it was the first time she had ever been in a gym. All around the room, people were exercising; some lifting weights, some using cross-trainers or treadmills, but all of them putting in the effort.

Lady Mary giggled and nudged my arm. 'Look, sweetie. That man has put a bottle of water in the Pringles tube holder.' I looked where she was pointing, to see a man on an elliptical trainer. I had to wonder if she was serious or not.

Barbie appeared from a side door just then, calling everyone to line up on the equipment. I didn't know what to expect from a bodypump class but as Lady Mary found a bench to the side to sit on, I lined off like the other people behind one of the barbells arranged on the floor. Then, Barbie had me stand in the front row, right in front of her as she faced the class of twenty.

'Warmup exercises,' she shouted. All around me, the class mimicked her movements as we began to stretch off. Then she had them all pick up their barbells to perform some slow movements that would prepare our muscles for the onslaught ahead. She used the word onslaught and that should have been warning enough, but I was still focused on being inspirational and on feeling incredible when the session was finished.

When Barbie had us do some deadlifts, Lady Mary cackled loud enough for us to hear over the music Barbie was playing to create rhythm for the class, 'It's the bend and snap move from Legally Blonde,' she guffawed. Barbie ignored her, yelled for everyone to get ready and counted down from five to one as she ramped up the energy in the room.

Looking back, I should have known that I was in trouble when I first walked in and saw that the average age in the room was somewhere under thirty. It was supposed to be a sixty-minute session but twenty minutes in I could feel my feet swimming around from the amount of sweat in my shoes and I would swear I smelled like a dump truck. At the front, Barbie was calling instructions and changing exercises every minute as she worked through a routine that she had either memorised or was making up on the spot based on what would hurt me the most.

'And thrusters!' she yelled as she hoisted the barbell above her head, lowered it to her shoulders and performed a squat. I tried one, saw sparkly lights dance before my eyes and gave up. As I staggered away to find water, Barbie glanced at me but did not stop what she was doing.

Instead, an assistant, a young man called Walter scurried across to make sure I was alright.

'I just need a drink,' I said as I pulled the top from my bottle.

'You are doing great,' he said enthusiastically. 'A real inspiration.'

'Uh-huh,' I grunted, leaning against a treadmill, and trying not to faint.

Behind me, Barbie called that it was time for a two-minute break. The class put down their barbells to get water and wipe off sweat. I looked at the hand towel I had to dry myself with and chuckled as it absorbed the moisture from one arm and was done. I needed a bath towel.

An athletic-looking woman in her late twenties snagged her water bottle from the floor next to me, 'Are you okay?' she asked. 'You don't look so good.'

I probably didn't look good. I probably looked like I was having a heart attack. 'I'm okay,' I lied. 'Really feeling the pump.'

'Okay, class, let's go!' yelled Barbie, taking up position again, her enthusiasm not even slightly dulled by the twenty minutes of exercise already performed. 'On three we go with a burpee into a snatch and press. Ready? One, two, three go!'

Somehow, the movements had got even more complex than they had been before. I was trying to copy the movements of everyone around me as they performed the action in perfect timing with Barbie and each other. I pushed the barbell above my head for what felt like the thousandth time, then barely kept control of it as I placed it back on the floor to perform a burpee. The barbell rolled as I flopped to the floor though, so my forehead clanged off it as I went down. No one seemed to notice so I shook my head, got back up and grabbed the barbell to flick it back up to my shoulders. As I pressed it above my head though, the sparkly lights came back. I heard someone gasp and realised I was off balance and moving across the exercise area guided by the weight above my head.

Someone said a rude word as I collided with them and fell on my butt. The barbell crashed to the deck somewhere behind me as the class screeched to a halt. I felt dizzy and very lightheaded, but I could hear Lady Mary laughing like she had seen the funniest thing ever.

'Are you okay, Patty?' asked Barbie.

'I think I just died.'

'No, you're still with us,' she replied.

'Really? Someone kill me, please.'

'Patty, you are so funny,' she chuckled. Then as I laid back and stared at the ceiling through confused eyes, I heard her ask if someone else was okay. Twisting around a bit so I could see, not far from me was a young Asian man sitting on the floor with blood all over his face and down his vest.

Oh, God. I had hit him with my barbell when I fainted.

## Eavesdropping

An hour later, once I was showered and changed and felt recovered, I packed a bag to go down to the sun deck. There would be hours of sun yet and I felt like sitting out in public rather than tucked away in the privacy of my terrace. George had been kind enough to give me one of his books, a signed copy of his most recent release. He wrote murder mystery stories that could be a bit graphic in places, but it was the type of book that I enjoyed even though I had never read one of his. In my bag was water and sun cream and my good sunglasses and an apple from the fruit bowl in the kitchen which was miraculously always full of perfectly ripe fruit.

'Does Madam require anything else?' asked Jermaine as I wrapped a sarong about myself and slipped my feet into a pair of slip-on sandals.

I shook my head. 'I don't think so, Jermaine. I plan to read and do little else for a few hours. I will take dinner here tonight if you would like to prepare something.' I knew that Jermaine liked to cook, I did too for that matter, but I had only let him prepare dinner for me a handful of times and I knew he wanted to do more.

He inclined his head in acknowledgement, a small smile playing on his lips. 'Is there something specific Madam would like?' he asked as I began toward the door.

Pausing to consider the question, I was interrupted by a knocking noise. I was a scant few feet from it, so I flashed Jermaine a cheeky grin and got there first because he was all the way across the room.

It was Barbie outside. 'Oh, hi, Patty. I'm glad to see you are alright,' she said, the words spilling out in a torrent as she came inside. 'You gave me quite a scare and the next thing I knew, you were gone. Hi, Jermaine.' As always, her brain was bouncing around from thought to thought, never pausing in between.

'Good afternoon. Miss Berkeley,' he replied, his formality purely for my benefit. He was so stiff as a butler that I found myself wanting to put a secret camera in the room to see how he acted when I wasn't around. Maybe I would catch him wandering around naked though, scratching himself and belching, so perhaps I shouldn't spoil the image.

I took a pace back to let her in as I said, 'Is that poor young man alright? Did I break his nose?' I could feel my cheeks warming again. I had been mortified to discover I had injured someone even though at the time I didn't have the balance to be able to get to my feet.

Barbie sucked in a breath as she nodded. 'It sure looked broken. Akihiko was very philosophical about it though; he said the universe balances itself out. I think he was suggesting that he was due it for some past crime.'

I was glad to hear it though the news did little to eradicate my sense of guilt. As the poor man was helped to his feet, Lady Mary had wished me luck and slipped out, commenting that she didn't think she would be following in my fitness footsteps after all. Guilt forced me to hang around for a while once I was able to stand up without the whirlies getting me, but the class had been abandoned so when my continuous apologies began to sound foolish, I had collected my things and slipped out too.

'Are you going to the pool?' Barbie asked, taking in my swimming costume and sarong with my bag hung over the crook of my arm.

'Yes?' I replied, hoping that was okay after whacking a person in the face less than an hour ago.

'I thought you were investigating the missing girl?' Barbie's face bore a confused expression.

'I have been. I'm just not sure what to do about it.' I wanted to say that I had realised I wasn't a detective and had no idea what I ought to do next. It wasn't as if I could start interviewing people and the likely culprit would be one of the unknown parties that forced their way on board last night. I didn't say that though; people were looking at me as if I had a special skill and I liked it enough to not want to burst my own bubble just yet. Instead, I said, 'I have already collected a good amount of information. Maybe a course of action will come to me if I just take my mind off it for a while.'

'Oh, well, okay, I guess that makes sense,' said Barbie. 'I really just stopped by to make sure you were okay. Have you had enough fluids and something to eat?'

I waved a dismissive hand. 'Barbie, dear, I am fine. I just got a little wobbly. You should give it no further thought.' Then I fished my sunglasses from my bag, opened the front door to my suite again and stepped outside, saying, 'If there is nothing else you need me for, I will see you both later.'

They both smiled and waved me goodbye as I left, breezily strolling along to the upper deck sun terrace where a pool boy would find me a lounger and position my umbrella just how I wanted it.

The pool area was busy, but there were loungers available as always. The sun terrace manager spotted me as I looked for him and he clicked his fingers to attract a junior member of staff. Two minutes later, I was happily reclined with my book in my hands and a fresh cup of ice water on the small table next to me. Endless blue sky stretched in every direction and the hot sun beat down to warm my skin as I settled in to read.

'Patricia, sweetie,' hissed Lady Mary right next to my right ear. I jumped out of my skin and was thankful I hadn't been taking a drink because it would have gone skyward. I placed my right hand on my heart to check it was still working and forced my tense muscles to relax again.

'Goodness, Mary. You made me jump.'

'No time for all that, darling. I've found the kidnappers.' She was whispering so no one around us would hear and crouching next to the lounger so her head was alongside mine. Then she pointed surreptitiously across the terrace, her finger flashing out meaningfully then disappearing again so no one would see it. 'Over there,' she whispered. 'The little guy with the huge henchman.'

I followed where she was pointing, and sure enough there was an easy to spot hulking great bear of a man. He looked like a wrestler from the TV except they all seem to be young men and this man had to be in his late forties. His head was shaved clean which just exaggerated the dangerous look his size implied, however, the tiny, bright yellow Speedo swimming trunks he wore made him look ridiculous. Beside him, and in direct contrast, was a small man. He had a moustache and a full head of red hair and looked to be Scottish perhaps from his milky white skin tone. Both men were facing us, sitting on the sun-loungers with their legs stretched out in front and the small man was talking animatedly while the giant next to him listened.

When she had me spend two hours looking for them fruitlessly this morning, I had been indulging her because she was a friend and because I thought she genuinely might have overheard something. By the time we gave up, my conclusion was otherwise. Looking at the pair of men now though, my imagination was filled with thoughts of the big man breaking bones on the smaller man's command.

'We need to call the police,' Lady Mary said.

Without taking my eyes from the two men, I replied, 'We can't. There are no police. We are in international waters and the ship is registered in the Bahamas.'

'Yes, yes,' she replied with a little impatience, 'I mean the ship's security. Mr Rutherford will know what to do.'

*I doubt that.*

I kept the thought to myself, but if I wanted to get the ship's security to do anything, I would need to be sure for myself. I began packing my things into my bag again. 'See the two loungers just behind them?' I indicated with my head.

'Yes?' replied Lady Mary, clearly not understanding what I had in mind.

Standing up and collecting my glass of ice water, I said, 'Why don't we sit there for a while? The sun is striking those loungers at a better angle, don't you think? Maybe we will hear something interesting.'

As realisation dawned, Lady Mary's face split into a grin. 'Goodness, Patricia, you are so adventurous. This is just like a spy novel, darling.' I started walking in a circuitous route to the target loungers. Lady Mary wasn't following though.

I went back for her. 'Lady Mary, are you coming?'

'Won't that look suspicious?'

'Suspicious? I don't follow.'

She glanced about to see who was watching or listening. 'The two of us just going over there and sitting down within earshot of them. Shouldn't we concoct a ruse for needing to sit there? Or have a conversation that they could overhear that would allay suspicion?'

'It's a popular pool area. There are people coming and going all the time. If we just sit and look like we are paying them no attention, they will pay us no attention too.'

Lady Mary did not look convinced, but she said, 'If you are sure, sweetie.'

This time when I set off, she trailed behind me. She began whistling though; something I had never heard her do and to my knowledge no one ever really does unless they are a cartoon character attempting to act innocent. Addressing her need to act the role of someone who was up to something while pretending to not be up to anything at all would just draw attention to us though, so I ignored it, reaching the two loungers directly behind the men a few seconds later.

Around the terrace, loungers were arranged in long rows, mostly in pairs with a small table in between for patrons to place drinks or other items on. We were now sitting directly behind the two men and facing the back of their heads. By sitting on the foot end of my lounger, I was less than three feet from their heads.

And I could hear what they were saying.

'How about a straight razor or a box knife, boss?' the large man said. His accent was Canadian, I thought, Toronto perhaps. When he said the word about it came out more like aboot, but I was basing my judgement on having once met a Canadian couple, so I wasn't ready to bet my life on his birthplace.

When the small man spoke, his accent was thick with something European. German or Austrian maybe underlying in the way he said some words, but his English was impeccable. 'No, no. It has to be something original. We want her end to be a surprise. She deserves that we craft a method of killing her that no one else would come up with, don't you think.'

'Sure thing, boss,' the large man replied.

'Maybe,' the small man began, pausing to consider his sentence before continuing, 'we need to draw it out. She has been in our lives for so long that I feel I owe her a slow death.'

I could feel my pulse quickening as I listened. These horrible men were discussing torturing someone to death as if it were a favour they were performing. It was terrifying. Was it Cari Gonzalez they were talking about? Had they murdered her bodyguards and stashed her in their room? A hand gripped my arm; Lady Mary was just as panicked as me.

Her eyes were as wide as saucers as she tugged my forearm to bring me closer. Meeting me halfway as we put our heads together to whisper, she said, 'What do we do?' her voice was an insistent, worry-filled squeak, betraying the same emotions I was feeling.

'I'm going to write that down,' the small man said in his European accent. 'We have some good ideas here now, Ramone.' Lady Mary and I both turned our heads and could see the man scribbling in a notebook, mumbling to himself as he did. 'So, we know where she is, why she has to die, and we have some ideas about how to kill her.' He shut the notebook and placed it on the table between them. A pen was sticking out the top where he had left it in the page he was writing on.

I needed to get that notebook!

'This is going to be our best work yet,' the man said cheerfully.

His henchman turned to smile at his boss. 'I think you are right, boss. This is like a dream come true, you know. Working with you, in this setting.'

The small man smiled back. 'You are too kind, Ramone. Um, Ramone, could you get me a drink?'

'Sure, boss. What would you like?'

'I don't know. Something fruity, but not with too much alcohol in it this time. Surprise me though, I need to pee.'

As the large man rose to his feet and snagged a wallet from a bag on the floor, the small man also clambered from his lounger. They were both leaving, and the notebook was still on the table! The small man left first, heading in one direction and Ramone moved away a few seconds later when he had shuffled his feet into a pair of green plastic flip flops.

My heartrate rising as I glanced about, I was about to seize my opportunity and steal the notebook.

'Oops! Almost forgot this,' said the small man to himself as he returned to claim the prize. 'Can't just leave it lying around where someone might steal it.'

'Goodness me, they are appalling men,' said Lady Mary when they were both out of earshot.

'We need to get that notebook,' I replied. 'There might be enough evidence in there for Mr Rutherford's men to act.'

'Can't we just tell him what we heard?' she asked.

I shook my head because I knew it wouldn't be enough. They could easily deny our claims and say we had misheard them. It was a noisy pool

– how sure were we about what we had heard? It would take no time at all to dismiss us. I needed something more concrete. I needed the notebook.

How to get it though? I needed a diversion that would distract the men for a minute, or maybe just a few seconds. Two men sitting by a pool – how do I distract them?

I asked Lady Mary. 'We could start a fire!' she replied excitedly. 'Or sound the alarm or maybe we should go over and chat them up. We are both attractive ladies, we can charm them and take the notebook while they are staring at our chests.'

I looked down at my boobs. They had given up being worth staring at a long time ago. Lady Mary had to be about the same age as me and her chest had done no better. Plus, we were each most of a decade older than the two men. But then I saw a younger woman in a bikini on the other side of the pool and it gave me an idea.

'Who are you calling, sweetie?' Lady Mary asked as I pulled out my phone and put it to my ear.

I held up a finger, begging a moment as the line connected. 'Barbie?'

Barbie's voice came on the line. 'Hi, Patty. Is it nice by the pool? Are you feeling okay still?' she asked.

'Hi, Barbie. Yes, it's lovely out and I feel fully recovered now. Are you busy?' I could hear a man's voice in the background, not that I considered it any of my business; I had something I wanted her to do but not if it meant interrupting something important to her.

'I'm with Jermaine,' she replied. 'We have been researching your gangster. You wouldn't believe some of the things we found. He is not a nice man.'

I believed her, but I had to ask a different question now. 'Barbie, why are you doing research?

'Oh, well, you made it sound like you could use some help, so Jermaine and I thought we might be able to look up background on Mr Perez and the missing woman. You know, just like we did with the sapphire,' she explained. 'What was it you called for?'

'I need a favour.' Lady Mary gripped my forearm again. The hulking henchman had returned, a drink in each hand. The brightly coloured cocktails looking incongruous in his massive mitts. A skull filled with blood might look more fitting. 'You might not like it though,' I breathed nervously into the phone. Then I explained what I wanted her to do.

Barbie said she needed a little while to get ready, which left Lady Mary and me to wait nervously, hoping that the killers one row in front of us didn't leave before she arrived. I say we were waiting nervously, but I think it was just me that felt trepidation. Lady Mary had taken one look at their cocktails and excused herself to visit the bar, returning a few minutes later with a glass for each hand. The first one was half empty before she sat down.

'That's much better,' she said as she drained the last of it, let the straw go and set it aside. 'A few of these and I shall be ready for anything.'

I doubted that would prove true.

The little while that Barbie needed to get ready turned out to be twenty-one minutes. She had undoubtedly had to hurry down to her cabin many decks below and return, but if she had rushed, there was no sign that it had made her sweat despite the rampant heat this afternoon. I spotted her as she came onto the terrace, her flowing blonde locks easy to spot.

She looked around until she spotted me, my hand raised to make the task easier, and she almost waved back until, with her hand half raised, she remembered that I wanted her to act like she was by herself.

Doing a good job of not looking like she was doing anything out of the ordinary, she began strutting toward the pool. I could hear her heels from where we were as they clip-clopped across the tiled deck. She had on six-inch killer pumps and the tiniest white bikini. Watching her move through the crowd was like watching the spectators in a tennis match as all eyes followed where she went. It wasn't just men though, women stared as well, though probably more from disbelief at her perfect hourglass figure and bouncing, orb-shaped boobs than from attraction.

She glanced in my direction once to make sure she was lining up in front of the right men, then turned to face away from them, looking across the pool. Her bikini was even smaller than I thought as the back of it was nothing more than a string. I couldn't even see it where it vanished between the cheeks of her perfect, toned bottom.

Then she bent over from the waist to place her bag on the floor and from around the pool I heard suppressed groans from a hundred men. I had to admit; it was quite a sight. As she straightened and turned around, she started fiddling with her bikini top, wrestling with the tie behind her neck as if it was annoying her, then it sprung open, forcing her to catch her boobs, one in each hand.

'Oops,' she said with a giggle. Then, looking at the two killers, she asked, 'Can I get a hand here, please?' Her voice was cute and demure and accompanied by an embarrassed smile as she bit her bottom lip. It suggested that men should forget their wives and children just to help her put her top back on.

Neither of the killers on the loungers in front of us moved, though there was a rush from around the pool as other men - dads, husbands, teenage sons, all ran to get to her first. I was eyeing the notebook, hoping to snag it when the two men got up, but they paid her no attention, as if the show in front of them held no interest.

As various other men converged on her, I saw Barbie's expression change from deliberately coy, to startled. Then her face vanished from sight as she was mobbed. I heard a cry of, 'Hey, no touching,' from her and hoped she would be okay. I wasn't getting that notebook though. A new tactic was needed.

Tapping Lady Mary on her arm, I said, 'Stay here. I'm going to create a diversion. When I do, grab the book and I'll meet you back at your suite.'

'What are you going to do?' she asked, her voice a mix of excitement and terror.

I swallowed, my throat dry from my own nerves. 'Something dramatic.'

Then I left her on her lounger, tucking my bag into the crook of my arm as I went. My childish plan was to get a pitcher of ice water and feign tripping as I walked in front of the killers so I could throw the cold water over them both. I was clumsy after all, so my plan ought to prove a cinch. I hurried to the bar, checking behind me to make sure the two men were still on their loungers and Barbie had managed to escape with her bikini intact. Her bikini top was back on, but a kerfuffle was brewing as she appeared to have slapped a middle-aged-looking dad for getting too handsy and now his wife was on her feet and getting involved.

At the bar, there were two pitchers of ice water on a tray ready for a waitress to take away. I grabbed one quickly while no one was looking and sped away again. Thankfully, the bar was close to the pool. It was in it, I suppose, actually, because it had a swim up bit to it on the other side, but the point is I didn't have far to go before I would be in tripping distance to get the two killers.

As I approached, I was looking at them, but trying to make it look like I was not looking at them. Achieving that though meant I wasn't really looking where I was going and was using the sound of the argument around Barbie to guide myself. She was still standing just a few feet in front of the killers, who were now at least watching the street theatre evolving before them.

'I saw you,' insisted the slapped man's wife. 'You grabbed her bum!' Her complaint was aimed at her husband, not at Barbie, but a third woman joined the fray.

'He wouldn't have been able to grab it, if it wasn't hanging out so much,' she pointed out. 'Why don't you put some clothes on, you slut?'

Barbie's jaw dropped open. 'Excuse me?'

The man said, 'Yeah.' As if he had seen a way to deflect attention from his butt-grabbing antics.

I lined up my jug of ice water. My route to the killers meant I would have to slip behind butt-grabby man, trip myself and dive forward. I glanced at Lady Mary, getting an encouraging thumbs up as a response. Then the wife of the butt-grabber took a swing at her husband, trying to slap his face. He danced back, right into my path, just as I was tripping myself. The jug of ice water bounced off his chest and went straight into my face. Momentarily stunned and unable to see, I bounced off his belly, stumbled, flailed my arms and fell backwards into the pool.

I felt myself going as my foot went out to correct my motion and found nothing beneath it. I hit the pool bum first but, actually, I didn't hit the water, I hit something else. It turned out to be a child's inflatable ring which my bum then wedged in. With my knees pressed against my boobs, and my natural buoyancy causing me to invert, I was trapped with my head below water and my bum sticking upward until a helpful hand grabbed my bum and gave it a shove.

I bobbed up to find Lady Mary standing at the side of the pool, looking down at me with a curious expression. Barbie was in the water next to me as was the butt-grabbing man who has clearly just claimed another butt: mine.

74

His wife looked incandescent as she began to berate him all over again. I backed away and climbed the steps at the end of the pool, thinking to myself that I should be glad I wasn't fully dressed. Then I remembered my bag. It had been in the crook of my elbow and had gone flying when I lost control. I spotted it, laying on the bottom of the pool a few feet from where I had fallen in. The pool staff and lifeguards were distracted trying to break up the wife and Mr Grabby as she had found a handy tray and was now trying to brain him with it as he attempted to get out of the water.

Barbie saw where I was looking, hooked my bag with a foot and joined me in escaping.

As Lady Mary joined us both at the far end of the pool, I saw that the killers were no longer sitting on their loungers. The poolside drama, or perhaps just the attention it had drawn was enough to scare them away. I looked about but there was no sign of them.

'What was that all about?' asked Barbie as we headed back to my suite.

I did my best to explain what Lady Mary and I had overheard. There being no need to embellish, I quoted verbatim some of their plans for Cari. She gasped in surprise a few times and joined in my disappointment that they had escaped.

'We should tell Mr Rutherford about the notebook anyway,' she said when I finished.

I nodded as I fished for my door card. 'I agree. Thank you for parading like that, by the way. I had no idea it would turn out like that. I expected they would jump up and help you.'

'Yeah,' said Barbie. 'They didn't even really look at me.'

The light on the door control switched from red to green and I pushed it open. I was dripping wet and my feet were squelching in my shoes. I needed to get dry and find some dry clothes. Barbie had so little clothing, it was probably already dry but as I thought that she fished her lycra sports gear from her bag.

'Do you mind if I use one of your bedrooms to get changed?' she asked.

'Got any gin, sweetie? I'm terribly parched?' asked Lady Mary.

'Would you like some afternoon tea, madam?' asked Jermaine, appearing silently in my living room from his attached cabin.

All three were facing me and waiting for answers. 'Barbie, of course, please pick one. Lady Mary help yourself or ask Jermaine to make you something. Jermaine, yes please, something herbal would be delightful. And get me Mr Rutherford if you would, please. Tell him I have news for him.'

'Very good, madam,' he replied as Barbie vanished into a bedroom and Lady Mary laid herself across a chaise lounge.

While everyone got on with something, I went into my bedroom and closed the door. It had been a busy day already, so I leaned against the closed door for a second, gathering myself, before pushing off to round the corner from the little corridor that led into the part where my bed was located.

Then I screamed. Or, at least, I tried to. The sound was cut off before it left my mouth because a hand clamped over it to silence me.

'No need for any of that, missy,' said a voice by my ear.

The hand had come from behind me as I entered the bedroom proper, but what had made me scream was the two men sitting on my bed. They were both close to retirement age; somewhere around their mid-sixties and had thinning grey hair and fine lines around their mouths and faces. They were clearly brothers, but not twins, the resemblance was there but if asked to guess, I would say there was a couple of years between them.

The one on the left said, 'That's enough now, Maurice. You can let the lady go. Mrs Fisher isn't going to cause any bother. Are you, Mrs Fisher?'

I stared at him dumbly as Maurice took his hand away from my mouth. I drew in a hard breath to yell for Jermaine, but the hand clamped back over my mouth again, stifling any noise I might want to make. I tried to bite at it but couldn't get any purchase.

'Mrs Fisher,' the same man on the bed addressed me, 'we intend you no harm. We just need to have a quiet chat with you.'

I nodded mutely. Unable to speak, and barely able to breathe with Maurice's giant hand covering my mouth and most of my nose, I had to convey my answer with my eyes. They probably demonstrated the panic I was feeling.

The man on the bed smiled and nudged his brother. 'You see, Roberto, I said she would be reasonable.' He kept his gaze fixed firmly on me when he stopped smiling to say, 'Now, Mrs Fisher, Maurice is going to remove his hand again. If you scream, I will have to silence you. I'm sure we would all rather avoid that, now, wouldn't we?' As he finished the sentence, he moved the bed covers to reveal a small handgun – the threat inferred but not spoken.

I nodded again and the hand slowly came away from my face. Sagging in place, my legs didn't feel like they could support me, and I suddenly felt dizzy from the adrenalin. 'I need to sit down,' I said as I began to topple.

Maurice caught my right arm and kept me upright until Roberto, acting like a gentleman, brought the chair from my dressing table. The other man, the one that did the talking, fetched a glass of water from the nightstand.

'What do you want?' I asked once I had taken a drink and the lights had stopped dancing in front of my eyes.

No one answered, at least not straight away. Maurice went back to his position near the door and the two older men took up their positions back on the bed. Then, once they were comfortable, the man whose name I had yet to learn spoke, 'All we want is the girl.'

I frowned at him. 'What girl?'

'There's nothing to be gained from protecting her or Eduardo, Mrs Fisher. I know my former allies do not have her. Nowak doesn't have the brain for it and Boris would have called me to laugh in my face if he had already succeeded in getting the prize. Plus, I know you are working for that pig Perez. So, my question is what did you do with her? She isn't hiding in your suite, we already searched. So, did you stash her in a cabin somewhere?'

'Do you mean, Cari?' I asked, still confused.

The man looked across the room to where Maurice was standing. 'Maurice, Mrs Fisher may need some additional motivation.'

'No problem, boss,' he replied, his voice a deep rumble that betrayed excitement at the prospect of *motivating* me.

I jumped from my chair to back away as he took a step toward me. 'I'll tell you everything,' I blurted. 'I just don't know anything. I haven't got the girl. I don't even know who she is and I'm not working for Mr Perez; I'm involved only in the interest of the ship.'

The man was not inclined to believe me, and he looked bored when he nodded to Maurice, telling him to get on with whatever it was he had planned. I wanted to scream for Jermaine, but I worried they would just shoot him when he came through the door.

As I hopped backward to keep some distance between myself and the advancing Maurice, I picked up the chair, holding it in front of me like a lion tamer.

The man on the bed said, 'Okay, Mrs Fisher,' as he held up one hand to allay Maurice's advance, 'let's say I believe you. You sound like an English dame, so tell me how you are mixed up with Eduardo the Cuban scumbag.'

Thankful that I now had a question I could answer, I said, 'I was invited to investigate what might have happened to her. That's all.' All three men now had a curious look to their faces, so I explained. 'There was an incident a couple of weeks ago with a missing sapphire. I was able to work out who had done what and solve the crime and now people act like I am some kind of super sleuth.'

'Hmm,' said the man on the bed. 'And you say that you refused to work for Eduardo?'

'Not exactly.'

'Well, now you work for me. I want to know where that girl is,' the man on the bed said.

I had to ask why; my natural curiosity demanded it. 'Why?'

'Because Eduardo has something that I want but he has too many men with him for an assault. At least according to the bodyguard we snatched earlier. The girl should provide some nice leverage.'

'You have one of Eduardo's bodyguards.'

'Had,' said Maurice.

'You let him go? I asked, confused.

Maurice just smiled at me. His boss answered though. 'You could say we let him go, yes. In a way: we let him go over the side. Something that could happen to anyone that doesn't give me what I want, Mrs Fisher.' He paused, then asked meaningfully, 'Can you swim, Mrs Fisher?'

I swallowed hard. Then, there was a knock at the door and Jermaine called out, 'Madam, Mr Rutherford is here to see you.'

Everyone froze for a second, then Maurice swatted the chair I was holding to one side, sending it across the room where it crashed into my nightstand.

'Is everything alright, Madam?' Jermaine opened my door so he could call to me. I couldn't see him because the door was in an alcove, but the change in volume told me he had heard the crash and was coming to investigate.

'Get out, Jermaine,' I yelled, believing he would assume I was naked and retreat back into the living area, but the unnamed man on the bed was too impatient to find out if he would, so he picked up his gun and squeezed off a shot that went through the partition wall Jermaine was behind. A curl of smoke escaped from the hole, and I could see light through it.

The noise of the shot in my bedroom was deafening, but I was able to hear Jermaine dive back through the doorway into the living area, letting me know he wasn't dead yet. Maurice was dissatisfied with that though, so he levelled his gun and shot a dozen holes through the wall between my bedroom and the living area. I had my hands over my ears to shield them from the sound, but the others didn't seem bothered by it.

'I think it is time to go, Roberto,' said the unnamed man as he stood up. 'We want that girl, Mrs Fisher.' Then he winked at me and said, 'You work for me now, remember that. We'll see you again real soon.' He dropped a card on the bed which displayed a phone number only.

From my suite I could hear shouting as Jermaine did his best to get everyone to safety. I had heard Barbie scream when the shooting had started but nothing from Lady Mary. Mr Rutherford was barking orders into his radio, but backup wasn't going to get here soon enough, the three men were leaving my bedroom and heading to where everyone else was.

In my living area Mr Rutherford bellowed, 'Stop right there.' It was followed by the sound of someone hitting someone else so, terrified of what I might find, I followed Roberto out of the bedroom.

Mr Rutherford was on the floor, holding his nose as blood seeped between his fingers. Maurice had hit him, then walked over him as both he and the elderly gangsters headed for the door. Across the room I could see Jermaine using his body as a shield for Barbie to hide behind and Lady Mary was still sitting on the couch with a glass in her hand. 'Caio, Mrs Fisher,' the nameless man said without bothering to look back. Just like that, they were gone, and the suite was quiet again. I looked around quickly; no one appeared to have a bullet hole in them. Maurice's shots had miraculously missed everyone, though I could see where several of them had buried themselves in the wood panelling or in one case, an oil painting.

On the floor, Mr Rutherford said a colourful word. I rushed to his side. 'I'm okay,' he said, starting to get up. 'I need to get some ice on this though.' He was holding his nose and looking more grumpy than scared.

On the couch, Lady Mary held her now empty glass above her head. 'Is there any more of this, Jermaine sweetie?'

I burst out laughing. I couldn't help myself. My life had turned ridiculous again. Then, half a dozen of the white-uniformed ship's security barrelled through my open door, screeching to a halt as they took in the scene.

From the couch, Lady Mary said, 'It's never dull around you, Patricia.'

'Are you alright, madam?' asked Jermaine. He looked dreadful, no doubt blaming himself for not preventing the men getting into my bedroom, but as I opened my mouth to reassure him, Mr Rutherford got there first.

'What were you doing this afternoon, then?' he demanded angrily of my butler. 'How did three armed men get into the suite that you are in charge of?'

Jermaine was embarrassed and crestfallen and ashamed and so many other negative emotions that he couldn't reply. But I could. Wheeling around to face Mr Rutherford, I said, 'Jermaine's task is not to protect my suite from invaders.' I asked a question I was certain I already knew the answer to. 'Did you leave the suite at any point this afternoon, Jermaine?'

'Yes, madam,' he replied slowly. 'I took your ball gown to the dry cleaners, and I had to buy ingredients for your dinner. They could have gained access during that time. I'm terribly sorry, madam, I should have checked your residence upon my return.'

I waved him into silence. 'Jermaine, I live in the suite. You do not. I accept that you will apportion blame on yourself, but I insist that it is unnecessary.' I swivelled back to face Mr Rutherford. 'There is nothing to be gained by assigning blame. Perhaps instead, you should be trying to chase the men who just left here.' My suggestion brought colour to his cheeks – he clearly hadn't thought to go after them.

Blood still coming from his nose, Mr Rutherford directed two guards to stay with me and took the others with him as he raced from my suite to see if the men could be spotted. I expected that it was too late.

Jermaine asked, 'Would you still like the tea I have prepared? It is four o'clock,' he pointed out.

'Tea? Yes,' I chuckled. 'Why ever not?' After all, it was four o'clock and my butler loved to honour British high society traditions.

'Who were those men, Patty?' asked Barbie, she had a hand to her chest as if trying to still her heartbeat. Jermaine had moved away from her as he went into the kitchen to fetch the tea and she was standing by herself now looking fragile.

I beckoned her to join me as I went to the couch. 'Let's sit, shall we?' I took a seat myself, slipping a handy throw cushion under me as I hadn't managed to get changed out my wet clothes yet. Barbie hadn't moved, so I patted the couch next to me and beckoned again for her to take a seat.

Lady Mary swivelled her head around. 'Have a drink, sweetie,' she said as Barbie began to move. 'It will calm your nerves.' When Barbie looked sceptical, she added, 'Look at me. I couldn't be any calmer unless I was asleep.'

Jermaine arrived with a small trolley he used for serving food. From it he delivered a pot of tea, three cups with saucers, plates and a three-tiered cake stand on which petit fours and a selection of delicate sandwiches were stacked.

He then produced a gin and tonic which he promptly handed to Lady Mary. 'Three more, please,' she said before she got the glass to her lips.

'That's a good idea.' I acknowledged, more to myself than to her.

'Oh. Would you like one? Those were just for me, sweetie.'

Jermaine returned a few moments later with a tray of glasses. I wasn't drinking much anymore, but I was indulging myself with an occasional gin so there were several very good bottles in the kitchen and Jermaine knew how I liked it. I hadn't intended to drink today, but my nerves were a little shot.

'What is it again?' Barbie asked as she tentatively sniffed hers.

It was Lady Mary that answered, 'My dear, Barbara. Gin is a distilled alcoholic drink that derives its predominant flavour from juniper berries.

In essence, it is vodka with an education as the only real difference between gin and vodka is the predominant flavour and aroma of the Juniper. In both, you start with a neutral spirit at 96% alcohol by volume that has been derived from an agricultural source like grain. With the gin, you then rectify or compound this spirit with a series of flavours known as botanicals, in such a way that the predominant flavour present is the juniper. Gin must, by law, then be bottled at a minimum alcohol by volume of 37.5%.' She finished her explanation, downed the rest of her glass and reached for another.

It was an impressive answer, perhaps demonstrating just how much of it she drank, but Barbie was still sniffing her glass. 'I don't usually drink,' she said, and I was just about to tell her not to, when she upended the glass and swallowed the lot in one hit like she was doing shots.

Lady Mary and I watched her silently for a second. She shuddered; a full-body event that seemed to start in her toes. When it stopped, she said, 'Wow.' Her voice somehow an octave deeper than a moment before. 'I might need another of those,' she added, her voice back to normal again.

'Are you sure?' I asked. 'You are always warning me about the danger of empty calories.' It must not be possible to have a figure like hers and eat anything that wasn't attuned to the person's nutritional needs.

'I do,' she conceded. 'But people keep trying to kill me when I am near you, plus this gin stuff tastes really good.'

'That's the spirit,' cheered Lady Mary.

'Well, just go easy. They are very high in alcohol, remember?' I warned.

A knock at the door heralded the return of Mr Rutherford. Getting punched on the nose had sparked some life into him at last, he had blood on the front of his perfectly white jacket where it had dripped from his nose and his eyes were already starting to blacken. 'They got away, I'm afraid,' he announced as he took off his hat. 'Can you tell me what they said or what they wanted with you, please?'

I explained that they were after Cari Gonzalez and seemed to think I would know where she was. When asked who they were, I had to shrug though. All I had was the names Roberto and Maurice; not a lot to go on.

When I finished speaking, Mr Rutherford said, 'This morning I had a report of a couple held in their cabin by three men. They forced their way in last night and wouldn't let them leave. They didn't harm them; it seems they just wanted the room to use. From the description the couple gave, I think it was the same men.'

'Do you think they are some of the men that came aboard by helicopter last night?' I asked.

'It seems likely, doesn't it?' he said with a nod.

Jermaine stepped a pace closer. 'Madam, I believe I can shed some light on the identity of the gentlemen that were in your room.' He instantly had everyone's attention. 'After you revealed that you were embroiled in the whereabouts of the missing Miss Gonzalez, Miss Berkeley and I took the liberty of conducting some research. Her fiancé, Mr Perez, appears to engage in several nefarious pursuits, though he has never been convicted of any. He owns several businesses in Miami, including a nightclub that burned down just yesterday.' He had been telling the truth about his nightclub I realised with surprise. 'He also owns a handful of bars, but the pictures revealed them to be in poor condition. Two of them, in fact, had been repossessed, suggesting that he is in some financial difficulty. We found several news articles alluding to his businesses, all of which were to do with the police raiding one of his premises or a person in his employ being arrested and convicted of a crime but denying Mr Perez had any involvement in or knowledge of their activities.'

'After Miss Berkeley left to join you at the pool, I continued my research, this time looking for known associates which is where I found the photographs of the two older gentlemen that were just here.' Jermaine stopped speaking to cross the room to the desk that held the computer. He clicked the mouse a few times and swivelled the screen. Both Mr Rutherford and I got up to join him.

We were interrupted by a knock at the door. Jermaine excused himself to answer it, disappearing from sight as he left the living area as Mr Rutherford drew his weapon and indicated to the other uniforms in the room that they should do likewise. Silently, he motioned for them to position themselves with strategic viewpoints of the door my butler was about to answer. I watched, holding my breath for a second but relaxed when I heard Jermaine talking to someone in a normal tone. The uniformed men also relaxed, their sidearms slipping neatly back into hip-mounted white-leather holsters.

On the screen was a photograph from a newspaper article. It was dated just nine days ago and carried the headline, "Crime bosses seen colluding." The reporter surmised that they must be up to something but was good enough to name the men in the picture. Roberto and Hugo Caprione were flanking Eduardo and there were four other men in the picture as they approached several black limousines, the doors of which were being held open by bodyguard-looking henchmen in suits. One of them I recognised as Maurice. I stared at the picture, trying to match the names listed with the men shown in it. Kasper Nowak was a name that came up several times in the article as was a man listed only as Boris.

Jermaine coughed politely to attract my attention. When I looked up, he said, 'Madam, there are two gentlemen here from maintenance. They wish to conduct repairs and inspect your suite to see if anything has been damaged.'

'I summoned them,' Mr Rutherford explained. 'I will leave extracting the bullets until we make port, and I can get a proper crime scene team in here. The holes are unsightly though and may have damaged your air-conditioning system where they penetrated the walls.'

'Of course,' I replied. Jermaine nodded to the men in their overalls, giving his permission that they enter my suite, but insisted they remove their footwear as, in his opinion, it looked dirty.

As the men put down their tools and got to work, I returned to reading the news article. The reporter posited three reasons why they might be meeting but went on to suggest that the most likely was to discuss how to fill the power vacuum now that underworld kingpin Dylan O'Donnell had suffered a heart attack and died. Dylan O'Donnell was described as a ruthless master of the criminal underworld and someone the Miami gangs had been working for out of fear for decades. The report concluded with a suggestion that Perez, the Capriones, Kasper Nowak, and Boris would struggle to pick a new leader and a battle for the top spot might ensue.

Dylan O'Donnell's name had a hyperlink on it, which took me to a separate article about his funeral. As it opened, my blood ran cold. 'Mary,' I called. She hadn't left the chaise lounge to join everyone else at the computer even though her gin was probably portable.

'Yes, dear?'

'Can you look at something for me, please?' I didn't really need her to confirm what I was looking at, but I was going to have her do it anyway.

'What is it, sweetie?' she asked as Barbie stepped aside to let her in. 'Oh. That looks just like the nasty little man by the pool.'

'Hmmm? Who looks like who?' asked Mr Rutherford.

The picture on the screen was Dylan O'Donnell but he wasn't dead at all. I had listened to him plot murder and torture by the pool this afternoon. He was a failed jockey that had chosen to pursue a life of crime, left his Dublin home in Ireland and found himself some years later rising through the ranks of the criminal underworld due to his ruthlessly murderous nature. The man I had seen had a different accent but that wasn't exactly hard to fake. Dylan O'Donnell was right here on this ship and could be behind everything that was happening. What I said, my voice a desperate and hushed whisper, was, 'He faked his own death.'

'Just like Elvis?' asked Barbie.

I chose to ignore her question, instead explaining to Mr Rutherford about the two men by the pool. As I spoke, one of his men lifted his lapel microphone to his lips, relaying a description of the two men and their names. By the time I had finished speaking he had already been able to confirm that there was no one on board listed under Dylan O'Donnell.

Uttering an expletive in his frustration, Mr Rutherford said, 'I'm sure a man like that wouldn't have too much difficulty faking some identification. We will circulate their description to all the staff. I expect they will be spotted at dinner, and we will be able to intercept them as they return to their cabin.'

I hoped it would be that easy. It niggled me though that a crime lord would fake his death and go on a cruise. Why would he do that? And why would he then kidnap and murder a woman? It wasn't making any sense, but then I told myself that I didn't think like a criminal.

Believing that Cari Gonzalez's kidnappers had most likely been identified, I breathed a sigh of relief. Everyone involved sounded thoroughly unsavoury and best avoided – the Caprione brothers and their henchman Maurice certainly were so I would be only too happy to leave their apprehension to the ship's security detail under Mr Rutherford and go back to having a less adventurous life.

'What will happen now?' I asked Mr Rutherford.

He tilted his head slightly as he considered his answer. 'I think that the captain will put directly into port. When I tell him that shots were fired in your suite today, he will most likely consider that passenger safety is in question, in which case he will not hesitate to act. However, with a ship this size it is not as simple as just calling ahead and turning up; we fit into less than one percent of the world's ports. We may have to carry on to Costa Rica anyway if there is nowhere else we can go. I will arrange for a very quiet and careful room by room search of the entire ship, but that will take more than a day to conduct so we need to hope we get lucky early on. Here's the problem though; even if we are able to apprehend the two men you have identified this evening or early tomorrow, we already know there are other violent people on board.'

'So, where are they?' asked Barbie.

Mr Rutherford shrugged as he said, 'Hiding out somewhere on the ship would be my guess. I need to go, if you will excuse me.' As he turned toward the door, he called out, 'Baker, Schneider, you will remain with Mrs Fisher as her personal escort and guard. I don't want anything to happen to her. Am I understood?'

Both men crisply replied with, 'Yes, sir.'

'Will that be necessary?' I asked.

He nodded grimly. 'I think it might be, Mrs Fisher. At least for now, just as a precautionary measure. At least until we find these men. I have one dead body and you said they boasted about putting another man overboard.'

'Yes. Will you be asking Mr Perez about that?' I enquired.

He twitched his nose as he thought. 'I am inclined to believe they were telling you the truth. Besides, I doubt Mr Perez would admit it if his men were going missing.'

I couldn't argue with his logic. Mr Rutherford excused himself again and left my suite.

'Begging your pardon, m'lady.' I turned to find the two maintenance chaps standing a few feet behind me. 'We're finished with our inspection. There's no damage to the air-conditioning that we can find, and the bullets, bar one, all appear to have been stopped by the outer walls of the suite. We will need to rip out the panels in some places in order to do a proper repair, but Mr Rutherford said we wasn't to do anything until we make port.'

'You said all the bullets, bar one. Where did the other one go?' I asked.

'Well, that's the bit of bad news, I'm afraid. That one went right through the controls for your oven.' I looked at it, only now seeing the hole for the first time. The oven was mounted on the far wall of my kitchen and was black so the hole in it was not obvious. 'We'll have to take it out and fit another, but I don't think we have a spare one on board.'

I wouldn't be having Jermaine prepare my evening meal after all. I said, 'Not to worry, gentlemen. Please arrange to conduct the repairs when you are able.' They mumbled an unnecessary apology, gathered their tools and shoes and left.

The two guards, Baker and Schneider, were hovering, both wondering what they ought to do now. I felt the right thing to do was act as a host and make them comfortable. 'Gentlemen, I have no plan to go out this evening other than for dinner. You should relax and watch some television or whatever you would normally do to relax. There is a games room if you are interested.' Amusingly, the games room was something I found by accident two days ago when I opened a door thus far ignored. Until then, I had thought it to be a closet.

'So, what shall we do now, Patricia?' asked Lady Mary.

As I considered the question and the two guards checked out the games room, Barbie tried to get off the couch. I say tried because she started to lever herself up, but nothing much happened. 'Um, my feet don't seem to work,' she slurred.

'How many of those gins did you have, Barbie?'

She looked at me, her eyeballs catching up a moment after her face turned. 'Two, I think. Might have been three.' Barbie's lack of body fat and rare intake of alcohol had rendered her distinctly tipsy after just a couple of drinks. 'I think I might like to have a lie down actually,' she said.

'You'll not be wanting this one then?' asked Lady Mary hopefully, as she selected the last ready-made gin and tonic on the table.

It occurred to me that I was still in my damp swimsuit, so excused myself to get showered and changed. By the time I came back out, Jermaine had settled Barbie in one of the spare bedrooms and Lady Mary had left. She had called through that she was going to see what George was up to before she went, so, finally, I was by myself.

With nothing to occupy me, I settled in front of the television and selected a film from the enormous library available. As it came on, I thought about the missing girl and had to wonder where she was and if she was safe. What was it that the Caprione brothers wanted her for? What would they do to her if they found her? Or did Dylan O'Donnell really have her? And would Mr Rutherford and his men find him before both he and his hulking henchman did her any harm. Settling into the depths of my couch with my feet tucked beneath me, I continued to ponder the strange day I had experienced, and my eyes began to feel heavy.

## Dinner

It was some time later when I awoke, making a snorting noise that startled me back to consciousness. Thankful that I was alone for my diabolical snoring, I stared out of my expansive window to appreciate the view. The sun had dipped and the bright sunlight that filled my suite when I sat down, was now reduced to a soft glow as the orange sun floated a few inches above the horizon. It was breathtakingly beautiful.

A polite cough came from across the room. I spun my head around in shock, terrified that I had uninvited guests again, then, to my relief, saw that it was my two appointed bodyguards, Baker and Schneider. How long had they been sitting there waiting patiently for me to wake up while serenading them with my snoring cacophony. As my cheeks flushed, I was glad they probably couldn't see me in the dim light.

'Will you be taking dinner, Mrs Fisher?' Baker asked.

'Dinner? I think I will just eat here,' I replied sleepily. Then I remembered my broken oven. I would be going out for dinner after all. I checked my watch to find that I had been asleep for two hours. I felt groggy and had to stifle a yawn as I stood up, one hand over my mouth and my eyes shut so that I almost lost balance and fell.

Twenty minutes later, with a swipe of lippy to compliment my tan, I left my bedroom to find my two white-uniformed escorts waiting for me in my living area. They were already standing and had their hats tucked neatly under their right arms. They looked ready to go, so I started walking toward the door that led out of the suite.

'I'll go ahead, Mrs Fisher,' said Baker as he slipped by me to get out the door first. 'Where is it that you would like to go?' he asked.

It was a good question but when I started to think about what I wanted to eat I remembered that the two gentlemen with me hadn't eaten either to my knowledge. 'Have you had dinner?' I asked.

'No, ma'am,' they replied automatically and in unison.

'Then please tell me what cuisine appeals to you. I will be happy with whatever you pick.'

They appeared surprised to be given the opportunity to choose, but their decision required only the briefest glance to pass between them. Then they both grinned and once again in unison said, 'Pizza!'

I laughed at them. 'Pizza it is. Do you have a favourite place?' I knew there was more than one place to get pizza on board.

Baker and Schneider led me to an elevator and down four decks to a mezzanine area where several of the ship's most intimate dining experiences could be had. I had eaten here twice but never at the cute Italian place they took me to. The mezzanine was set out to resemble a village square with shops and restaurants. There were chairs outside the restaurants where many guests were drinking wine and enjoying the food. It was mostly couples, but I spotted one or two families with younger children.

We ordered food and sparkling water. The men couldn't drink anyway so I abstained for their benefit even though they told me there was no need. To pass the time, I asked Schneider about himself, learning that he was Austrian and the youngest son of a man that was the chief of police in his hometown. He described home as a beautiful place in the shade of the Alps where most people were employed in the cattle and farming industries. His three elder brothers were all in cattle and spent their lives moving cattle about. He hadn't wanted to do that, and in a rebellious moment, when challenged to find something else to do in the area, he had signed up to work on a cruise liner, leaving a landlocked nation for a life on the oceans. He had no regrets.

In contrast, Baker was from a seafaring family and had no siblings. He hailed from Northern Ireland, a small town on the coast called Ballykinloss where many town folks were fishermen. He had never questioned what he would do when he was old enough but had also surprised his family with his decision to leave home to work on a cruise line.

We ate delicious pizzas and chatted for almost an hour. I was still tired though, my fatigue most likely caused by several bouts of terror and the insane bodypump session I had all but died from. It wasn't necessary to prompt the men to take me back to my suite, Baker saw me stifling another yawn and led me back to the elevator.

As the elevator ascended, it pinged and slowed though we had not yet reached our floor. We were two below it on number eighteen where other people wanted to get on. The car could comfortably hold twenty so there was plenty of room as two couples in their early forties, dressed for a night of dinner, dancing and entertainment got on. There was a nightclub and a cabaret place on the next deck down, the very place I had seen the illusionist, in fact.

Then I spotted him, standing out because his hulking frame put his head above the crowd of people: it was henchman Ramone from this afternoon! Just as the elevator doors started to close, I dived through them, impulse moving my feet without me consciously deciding it was the right thing to do.

'Mrs Fisher!' I heard Baker squeak in surprise as the doors shut behind me, trapping my escorts inside. There were more than one hundred people in sight, but I felt quite exposed and alone suddenly. The hulking Ramone was talking to someone unseen, however as people between us moved, I spied his boss, Dylan O'Donnell. They were moving toward me, heading for the bank of elevators I had just left and dressed for a casual dinner in shirts and trousers, maybe taking an early meal so they could get back for more torturing before bedtime. The horrifying thought popped into my head like a bad joke, but they were still coming toward me, and I had nowhere to go.

Telling myself to calm down, I turned around and pressed the button for the elevator. I didn't know what else to do, but there was no reason for them to believe I was anything other than a lady on her way back to her cabin. As they arrived next to me though, I remembered that the Caprione brothers had known who I was. Maybe these two would as well!

Ramone pressed the already lit call button, his finger twice the diameter of the button itself. I swallowed hard and told my legs to stay steady. I could act like I just changed my mind and walk away rather than get into a lift with two seriously deranged and dangerous men who might already have me listed as a target, but before I could move my feet, Ramone leaned down and spoke to me.

'I know you,' he said gently, like it was a promise.

Slowly, I turned my head to face upwards toward his, terror gripping me as my worst nightmares came true. I had inadvertently slipped my bodyguards and now the killers had me. I was going to have to scream to get attention and hope they didn't shoot everyone and drag me into the elevator.

Nothing happened for a beat. Then he broke into a huge grin. 'You're that dame that fell in the pool this afternoon,' he roared with laughter. 'I thought I was going to have a hernia; I laughed so hard.'

Dylan O'Donnell tutted. 'Ramone, you are being impolite to the lady. You should apologise.'

Ramone brought his laughter under control, tears leaking from the corners of his eyes. As he wiped them away, he said, 'Please excuse my manners.'

The lift pinged and I had to make a decision. They both got on, I hesitated, then Ramone held the door for me, and I saw little option other than to nod graciously and join them.

'What floor?' the tiny boss man asked.

Cursing myself, I tried to guess what floor they might be heading to and said, 'Twelve, please?'

'Ah, down in the depths like us pair then.' He didn't expand on his statement but when he only pressed the one button, I surmised that I had guessed right. Not exactly a million to one shot, since there were only sixteen decks with accommodation, but a lucky guess, nevertheless.

The elevator stopped twice to let other people on and off, arriving at deck twelve just a couple of minutes later. Once again, Ramone held the door so I could depart first. For a thug that like to cut up women, he was able to act the gentleman when it suited. I was stuck with the same dilemma as before though; I had three choices of direction and no idea which one they would pick. If I could pinpoint which cabin they were in, maybe I could find out just who it was they planned to torture to death on this trip.

I chose to go right, but my luck didn't hold. They went straight and I had to wait before I went after them because, gentlemanly or not, they were still deadly killers, and I didn't want them to think I was following them.

I counted to ten, then came back to the elevator and went the way they had come. There was no sign of them though. I searched for ten minutes, going back to see if I had managed to get it completely wrong and they had chosen the passage to the left, but whether they had or not, they were nowhere to be seen.

I had lost them and any hope of finding out who they were planning to kill.

I made my way back to the elevator and rode it back to the twentieth floor. People, mostly couples, got on and off at various floors but no one tried to kill me or do anything threatening so I arrived unmolested on the top deck still irked that I had let Dylan O'Donnell and his henchman get away. I needed to find Mr Rutherford and warn him about them now. Maybe his men would be able to knock on doors until they found them.

'Mrs Fisher!' called a voice loudly over the hubbub of the guests circling around me. I was on my way to the top deck restaurant, the one that had to be booked by reservation by all except a few select suites, one of which was, of course, mine. I hoped to find Mr Rutherford there but was confident that I would at least find a senior member of the crew who would be able to contact him for me.

The voice belonged to Baker. I turned toward the shout to see both he and Schneider jogging through the bustling guests. As he breathlessly caught up to me, he said, 'Mrs Fisher, thank goodness. You gave us quite the scare.'

I got the impression they had been frantically searching for me and circling around and up and down between the decks in their bid to relocate me. I didn't have time to apologise though. 'I spotted Dylan O'Donnell. He was going back to his cabin. I need to find Mr Rutherford now.'

Baker looked like he wanted to ask questions, but Schneider said, 'I'll get him.' He spoke into his lapel microphone, the message he gave was that the duty watch commander was needed for an urgent matter. Then he ushered me toward the top deck restaurant where he believed we might find him anyway.

We barely got three paces though before the captain's distinctive voice cut through the airwaves. 'This is the captain. Report.'

Schneider gave a brief explanation, telling the captain what I had told him about Dylan O'Donnell, the man Mr Rutherford should be looking for and finished by giving him our current location. The captain listened, then instructed him to request that I wait for his arrival - the captain himself was coming.

We didn't have to wait long. Less than two minutes later a door opened to our right spilling half a dozen white-unformed crew and the handsome Captain Huntley into the crowd moving about on the deck. Being recognised by many, the captain had to smile and greet people as he passed through them, but I was moving toward him feeling there was no time to lose.

'Mrs Fisher,' he said when we were close enough for conversation. 'I understand your day has been interesting.'

I chuckled at his turn of phrase. 'That it has, Captain Huntley. Thank you for coming yourself.'

'Mr Rutherford needed rest,' he replied. 'He has been on the go for almost forty hours and broke his nose earlier today, but you know about that of course. Now, tell me, please. What is it that you need me to do?'

I explained about spotting the hulking Ramone and his tiny boss, Dylan O'Donnell and about what I overheard by the pool. I explained why I believed they might have a young woman stashed in their cabin that they intended to harm. Since there was only one reported missing person on board, it was a logical conclusion to assume it was Cari Gonzalez. I didn't say that though, the glance that passed between us was enough to tell me he had reached the same conclusion.

'Please show us where you lost sight of them, Mrs Fisher,' he requested, after which we were all moving; eight guards plus the captain and one middle aged woman. It made me feel like Princess Leia surrounded by stormtroopers as we hurried through the ship.

Soon enough, we were back outside the elevator on the twelfth deck. 'This is where I lost them,' I admitted. 'I believe they went straight on but I might have that wrong so they could have gone left. I went right so they didn't go that way and they were nowhere to be seen just a few seconds later so they must be in one of the cabins at the start of the passage.' Ahead of us, a long passage stretched down the ship, cabin doors appearing every twenty feet or so in pairs so the rooms behind them would be pairs that were mirror imaged.

'Please wait here, Mrs Fisher,' the captain requested, then left a guard with me just in case as he took his security detail and knocked loudly on the first door he came to. On the other side of the passage, another officer did the same thing.

With nothing that I could do for the moment, I wandered a few feet away to the edge of the ship. The passage going straight ahead would have cabins facing the sea on the port side so to my left was a pair of doors that led outside. Unlike my suite, where I enjoyed a private balcony, at this level the cabins had portholes that looked out to allow light in. The last traces of the sun were dipping into the waves on the horizon as I peered out.

Then I spotted them. Fifty yards away, the distinctive little and large silhouettes of Ramone and the diminutive Dylan O'Donnell were framed with the sun behind them. They were standing at the railing and looking out to sea.

Was I too late and they had already killed her and were now contemplating their success? Sickened by the thought, I pushed the door open. The guard the captain had left with me called for me to stay, but I swung my head to look at him with urgent eyes and pointed. As I let the door shut behind me, I could hear him relaying an urgent message to the captain through his radio.

I walked toward the killers, confident that I was about to be joined by eight armed men. I was awash with a sense of anger. A long day had not yet led to the successful recovery of Miss Gonzalez, and I wondered if the captain had found the killers' cabin and was staring right now at her ruined body.

Then, as I closed my distance to them, they moved. Ramone's tiny boss turning toward his muscled protector and standing on his tiptoes to kiss him lightly on the lips.

Wait, what?

As the kiss broke, the dying traces of the sunset shone between them, and I could see they were holding hands. My brain didn't get to join the dots though because shouting behind me heralded the arrival of the captain and his men as, weapons drawn, they shouted for the two men to get their hands in the air.

Clearly shocked and bewildered, the two men froze.

The captain came to stand next to me. 'Well done, Mrs Fisher. You have a nose for finding people that do not want to be found.' I couldn't respond though; I was watching the horror and surprise on the killers' faces.

'Get down on the deck and place your hands out to your sides,' barked the lead officer.

'Ramone! Ramone, what's happening?' squeaked the tiny crime lord.

The huge henchman replied with, 'I don't know, boss. We better do as they say though.' Slowly the two men separated and sunk to their knees. That was as far as they got though as the security detail swooped in to flatten them, checking them for weapons and cuffing their hands behind their backs as they lay on the cool deck.

'We were just watching the sunset,' Ramone complained. 'We haven't done anything.' They were not acting like seasoned career criminals.

With dread forming in my stomach, I said, 'I think I may have made a mistake.'

Next to me, the captain pursed his lips and sniffed. 'How so, Mrs Fisher? You advised me that you overheard these gentlemen plotting to kill and dismember a woman earlier today.'

'That is what I heard. I'm just not sure…' I trailed off what I was saying, crossed the deck and knelt next to the tiny boss man.

'By the pool today, I heard the two of you discussing how you were going to murder Cari Gonzalez today. What have you done with her?' I demanded.

They exchanged a glance, then the boss said, 'Who's Cari Gonzalez?'

'We were plotting the end to our screenplay,' said Ramone.

'We're writers,' added the boss man.

'You're writers?' I echoed, struggling to believe what I had just heard.

'Yeah,' they both replied together.

'Well, writers and actors,' added Ramone.

'Then how come you always call him boss?' I asked triumphantly, thinking I had caught them out.

Ramone tutted. 'Because that's his name. Boswell Brinks. He's published a load of books under that name too, you can look him up.'

Boswell. I had heard him calling the man, Bos, not boss.

'What cabin are you in?' the captain asked.

'16350,' Ramone replied.

The captain nodded at one of his men. 'Take the cuffs off, please, Lieutenant Chivers. It would seem I owe you both an apology.' As the captain stepped forward to help the man up and shake their hands in a show of his sincerity, I tried to fade into the shadows. I was mortified. Who did I think I was? I had let myself be convinced I was some kind of super sleuth that could crack the kidnapping, find the girl and save the day. The result of my interference was my friends being shot at, Barbie getting felt up and now I had caused a nice couple to be terrified and traumatised. The cherry on the top was how I had caused embarrassment to the captain, a man that had shown me nothing but respect and kindness.

I wanted to run back to my suite so I could hide my face but I remained where I was so I could take my medicine.

As the security guards led the two men back to their cabin, the captain still apologising and discussing ways in which he would make amends, I was forgotten. I thought they were all going to just leave me there, but Lieutenant Chivers paused at the doors to deliver a message. 'The captain will see you tomorrow, Mrs Fisher.' Then he too ducked inside, leaving me feeling small, foolish and alone. At least I knew why they hadn't been distracted by Barbie's show earlier.

For the first time in two weeks, I thought about my husband Charlie. I needed a shoulder to cry on and I didn't have one.

## Morning

Sleep had come fitfully, the happy contentment I had enjoyed for the last two weeks replaced by guilt, embarrassment and a continuing theme of self-beratement. By the time I got back to my suite, Barbie had left, the gin slept off over a few hours in one of my spare rooms, but Jermaine had been waiting for my return in case I needed him for anything. Thinking back now, I couldn't even remember what I said to him, but it had been no more than a few words as I glumly took myself to bed. I hadn't even said goodnight to Baker and Schneider or spoken to them at any point as I walked back to my suite last night.

Now, the sun was shining through my bedroom window like it had no cares in the world, its perpetual warmth like an optimistic fool I wanted to slap. The dominant emotion keeping me awake last night was anger; anger at myself for thinking I could help. Who was I kidding?

Feeling despondent, I stayed in bed, staring at the ceiling and wondering what I could do today that would improve my mood. I dozed but was awoken by the sound of voices coming from the living area. The sound far louder than it normally would be because I now had a dozen holes in the wall between the rooms through which the sound was travelling.

Though I couldn't make out the words, the tone of the conversation concerned me enough that I forced myself out of bed to see who was there. Thankfully, I caught sight of myself in the mirror before I left my bedroom, delaying long enough to at least tidy my face and hair.

'Madam, good morning,' Jermaine greeted me. His tone was grave, and his expression matched it. The person he was talking to was Mr Rutherford, but Baker and Schneider were also there, already up and dressed. They all greeted me at the same time.

'Good morning,' I replied with a wave. 'What's going on?'

Mr Rutherford spoke first, 'Please forgive another early morning intrusion, Mrs Fisher. I'm afraid there has been some developments.'

Curious, I asked, 'Such as?'

He took a second as if trying to work out how best to frame what he wanted to say. 'Lady Bostihill-Swank didn't return to her suite last night and no one has seen her since she left here.'

I felt the colour drain from my cheeks even as a fleeting hope that she had shacked up with the Swedish cocktail waiter from the pool flitted through my mind. I dismissed the notion. She had been taken; I was certain of it.

Jermaine darted forward to steady me as I backed toward a couch to sit down. I felt dizzy or lightheaded - however you wanted to describe it, I was off-kilter. 'Which port are we going to?' I asked, remembering that he had said the captain would interrupt the journey if he believed the passengers might be in danger.

'Cayman Islands,' he replied. 'It is the only port anywhere near us where we will fit and doesn't already have a cruise ship at dock. We should arrive some time tonight.'

My mind was whirling still from the news that Lady Mary was missing. What possible motivation could anyone have for taking her? The same question had to be applied to Cari though. Since I had proven my original theory that Dylan O'Donnell had her was incorrect, I was back to having no idea who might or why. Someone had taken her, the Caprione brothers wanted her because they wanted something from Eduardo that he would be unwilling to give them. Were they the only ones that had come aboard though? If the rival gangs, which had seemed united in the picture Jermaine had shown me, were now fractured, had they followed Mr Perez to the ship and taken his bride? To what end? I doubted it was for the reason Eduardo had given me; the lie about being forced to sell his nightclub and then setting fire to it.

'I need to speak with Mr Perez,' I said getting up. The sense of defeat I had felt last night and when I awoke this morning wasn't gone, but whether I was a ridiculous woman with ideas above her station or not, my friend was missing, and I had to find out why. Maybe I couldn't help, but I was going to try.

'I think it would be best if you remained in the suite until we have made port, Mrs Fisher,' said Mr Rutherford. 'The Caprione brothers already showed an interest in you. I have no desire to expose my men,' he indicated Baker and Schneider standing just behind him, 'to any further danger.'

'Yes,' I replied. 'You should take them away.'

'Take them away?' he repeated. 'They would be better employed keeping you here.'

As my eyebrows shot to the top of my forehead, he stood up and backed away, wide eyes showing that he knew he had said the wrong thing. 'Are you proposing to place me under house arrest again?' I asked, my voice raised so I was almost shouting.

'No. No, not at all, Mrs Fisher.' He was holding up his hands in defence.

'I should think not. Now, if you have nothing further, Mr Rutherford, I suggest you vacate my cabin so I can get dressed.' The three men in white uniform exchanged embarrassed glances, then mumbled apologies and started toward the door. I made them stop when I asked, 'What are you doing about Lady Mary, Mr Rutherford?'

'Um,' he replied. 'I haven't really...'

'That's what I thought,' I snapped, cutting him off. I had suffered enough of his ineptitude. 'You need to find the criminals on board this ship and take them into custody.

'No one knows where they are,' he whined.

'You have hundreds of staff working in public areas; these men are not invisible. Circulate their descriptions and have everyone looking for them. Get some gumption man!'

'But only the Caprione brothers have shown themselves, if there are other parties aboard, they have failed to reveal themselves. No one knows what they look like.'

'What about the internet? We know their names. Assuming it was Kasper and Boris and whomever else that arrived last night, then you have a short list of pictures you need to find. I expect Google will be very helpful.'

'What if they are hiding?' he asked, his voice quiet.

I fixed him with a hard stare. 'I bet I find them.'

He nodded meekly. 'I bet you will.' He twiddled his hat and stared at the carpet for a few seconds, then he said, 'I'll get those descriptions circulated.' He turned and bumped into Baker and Schneider, the three men then fumbling to get to the door and escape my sight.

Suddenly, I was alone. 'Would you care for some breakfast, madam?' asked Jermaine, reminding me that I wasn't alone at all.

'Yes, thank you,' I replied absently after a moment of thought. My brain was stuck on the problem I now faced. Mr Rutherford was basically an idiot, my friend was missing, and I was willing to bet that one of the gangs of hoodlums had her. No one was coming to help her any time soon. It occurred to me that I had just said yes to breakfast as if I was going to sit down for a nice meal and read the paper while Lady Mary was held captive somewhere. 'On second thought, Jermaine,' I said, 'I'll take a banana to go. I need to find Lady Mary.'

'Then I will come with you, madam,' he replied.

'Okay. You will need to change. Butler clothes will be inappropriate for talking to gangsters.' He nodded in agreement, selected a banana from the fruit bowl on the kitchen counter, which I had to swipe from his hand before he attempted to peel it for me, then headed to his cabin to get changed.

The second he was out of sight, I quietly let myself out of the suite's main door and hurried away. I needed to be out of sight before he realised I had left him behind. I had no idea what I was walking into, but I did know that I wasn't going to let Jermaine put himself in danger. The men I needed to speak with, the men that I believed had Lady Mary, were dangerous men. I was a middle-aged, small English woman they would associate with their mothers or their aunts or some other harmless female relative. Jermaine was a tall, relatively muscular man. They would see him in an entirely different light.

'Mrs Fisher,' the shout came from behind me, arresting my motion. It wasn't Jermaine though; it was Baker and Schneider. They must have been lurking around the corner from my suite because they were onto me before I had gone two paces from my door.

'You can't stop me, gentlemen.' I said as I turned to face them. I felt ridiculous trying to stare them down in my pyjamas and dressing gown, but I gave it a go anyway.

'No, we want to go with you, Mrs Fisher,' Schneider explained.

Baker added, 'It's... well, it's not that we don't support Mr Rutherford, but he seems...'

'A little lost?' I asked, providing a word that I felt suited the end of his sentence.

'Something like that,' Schneider conceded. Then he said, 'Mrs Fisher, there are people in trouble, this ship is our home, and we are supposed to be the ones ensuring the security of the guests and staff on board her. If you are going to try to help, then we want to support you.'

I looked at the two men. They were young, but they were men and neither one was what you might call small. Indeed, they were muscular and dynamic, plus they were armed. Having them to watch my back again sounded like a positive move. The gangsters wouldn't like them, nevertheless, my gut reaction was that they would prove useful.

'I have to see Lady Mary's husband,' I announced as I turned to go, hurrying away again for fear Jermaine would find me if I hung about any longer. So, with my bodyguards in tow, I went in search of answers.

## George

'Oh, thank goodness you are safe, Patricia!' George said as he pulled me into a hug at his door. 'When I couldn't get you on the phone all night, I feared you had been grabbed as well.'

Of course he had been trying to call me. If Lady Mary was nabbed coming back from my suite yesterday evening, then he had last seen her not long after lunchtime yesterday. She had been with me since I went to the pool.

'My phone went into the pool,' I explained. 'I think it is toast, so I didn't get any of your calls or messages.' As I broke the embrace, I could see his eyes were welling up. 'Oh, you poor thing,' I said. 'You must be worried sick.'

George backed into his suite, beckoning for us to come in as if he had suddenly remembered his manners and realised we were standing on his doorstep. 'I don't remember the last time Mary and I spent a night apart. Mary thinks I can't manage by myself so she will be worrying about me even though she is the one in trouble.' His voice caught as he said it, breaking my heart with his concern for his wife.

I sat him down on a nearby couch, Baker and Schneider continued to hover by the entrance as I said, 'George, is it possible she is just with someone else?' He gave me a horrified look as if the suggestion was mad. 'Could it not be that she just had one too many last night and is asleep on someone's couch?'

He shook his head vigorously. 'Mary doesn't make friends. You are the first person I have seen her latch onto like this in years. Wherever she is, she is not there willingly. Is there anything you can do to help me find her?' he was asking the question not of me, but of the two security guards standing mutely near the door.

They just looked at me. As I turned my gaze back to George, I said, 'I have met two of the criminal gangs already, George. I even know which suite one of them is staying in. Shortly, I am going to ask some questions.'

'Oh, thank, thank you, thank you so much,' he gushed.

'I need to borrow some of Lady Mary's clothes.' At my request, George looked at me properly for the first time, finally noticing that I was wearing my night clothes and dressing gown.

He was polite enough not to ask why. 'Of course,' he replied. 'Please help yourself.'

Ten minutes later, I had on an odd collection of items because very little of her wardrobe fitted me. She was a dress size smaller than me and most of her clothes were fitted items from Channel or Dior or some other expensive designer label it would never occur to me to even look at because my legs would go weak from one glance at the price. Her feet were a size smaller than mine too, so I rejoined the three men in the suite's main living area wearing a pair of white Gucci running shoes that I had found in a box. They looked like they had never been worn and though they pinched my toes a bit, they were the only shoes of hers I could get on my feet. Paired with it, I had a loose flowing yellow skirt and a mauve roll neck sweater that had no place being worn in the Caribbean. It was all I could find that would fit so I avoided looking in the mirror because I knew I looked ridiculous. Then I remembered my hair and rummaged again to find a hat of some kind. She didn't have one, but George did. He had a selection that he used to protect his balding scalp. None of them would go with anything I was wearing but a baseball cap tucked away at the back was the least offensive choice.

The men all looked at me, their eyes bugging out a little as they took in my wardrobe choices though their comments remained unspoken.

'Shall we go?' I asked Baker and Schneider as I crossed the room.

'Should I come with you?' George asked, probably feeling a little odd at being left behind.

I shook my head though. 'Far better if you stay here in case she does return.'

He nodded by way of reply though I think he was happy to have an excuse to stay where he was. There being nothing left to say, I gave Baker a *let's go* look and we left poor George behind to worry.

Eduardo Perez's suite was a deck down and half a ship over, a ten-minute walk at least but swifter than usual because it was still early and there were very few people up and about to get in our way. It was something to be thankful for, given the stares my outfit drew from the few early morning joggers we did see.

Despite the odd looks, we arrived at Mr Perez's suite to find the door open. I got a sense of dread as we approached, imagining a scene inside akin to the Valentine's Day massacre. That wasn't it though, one of his dark-suited bodyguards was standing just inside, looking intentionally dangerous as usual.

'Good morning,' I said. 'I'm here to see Mr Perez. Is he at home?' The answer was rhetorical as I could see him in the main living area beyond the guard.

The bodyguard in his dark suit didn't reply though, he looked over the top of my head to lock eyes with Baker and Schneider as a macho competition of who has the meanest look took place. Each man was staring, silent and unblinking. If there were rules to the contest, I didn't understand them, so, bored, I saw my opportunity and slipped through the gap between bodyguard and wall.

'Mr Perez,' I called to get his attention.

'Hey!' said the guard. He was behind me now though and had to deal with Baker and Schneider as they too made their way inside.

Other guards, those standing closer to Mr Perez saw our intrusion and moved to intercept until Mr Perez spoke. 'Stand down,' he commanded. He was looking at me as the uncomfortable tension between his men and mine grew. 'Mrs Fisher, so good to see you this morning. You don't appear to have had any success in finding my fiancée.' His tone was aggressive, which combined with the hard stares coming from half a dozen of his bodyguards made me feel quite queasy with nerves.

Looking about though, there were significantly fewer bodyguards than there had been. 'You have enemies on board,' I said softly, keeping my eyes locked on his as I tried to impart sympathy. I needed him to cooperate. 'I am not one of them. One of *my* friends has been taken now,' he had the decency to look surprised at my news, 'but I don't understand what is going on and why everyone is after Cari. Will you please tell me what it is that they want her for?'

'I already told you,' he replied.

'But that wasn't the truth, was it?' I accused him openly.

Several of his bodyguards took a step forward and one said, 'She just called you a liar, boss. Let me cut her.' His hand flicked out, a knife suddenly in it.

Then, the tension in the room that had been threatening to bubble over, erupted as Baker and Schneider went for their side arms. I damned near wet myself when Mr Perez shouted again. But as he called for his men to halt before a close-quarter gun battle started, I spun to face Baker and Schneider, grabbing their arms even as they tried to draw their guns.

With everyone in the room poised to kill, Mr Perez sounded bored when he said, 'Mrs Fisher, all you need to know is that one of the enemies you allude to has my future wife and now possibly your friend it would seem.'

'That's not good enough, Mr Perez. I know that Dylan O'Donnell died and left a gap in the organised crime structure.' He looked surprised that I had connected some of the dots. 'I also know that your group,' I indicated around the room, 'are just one of several gangs that might now attempt to claim the dominant position now available. What I don't know is why you are being pursued by them or why they would take Cari. Please tell me why,' I begged.

Mr Perez had his head down in thought for a moment. When he raised it, he said, 'Mrs Fisher I am not used to being questioned and I don't remember ever tolerating anyone calling me a liar.' I swallowed hard. 'You are right though that I lied about my... profession. All you need to know is that I have something that the others want and one of them has taken Cari to force my hand.'

'What is it that you have?' I asked.

He bowed his head again and shook it. 'That is not something that you need to know.'

'What does the ransom note mean. At least tell me that. I have nothing to go on,' I begged.

117

He met my eyes again. 'I genuinely do not know what the ransom note means, Mrs Fisher. Nor do I know who wrote it.' I believed him for once. Despite everything else, he actually looked concerned about his bride-to-be and gave me the impression he would tell me anything if he knew it – except what it was that they were after. I had already begged for the information though; I wasn't going to do it again.

'Is there anything else you can tell me, Mr Perez? Anything that will help me locate the men that have taken my friend?'

'No, Mrs Fisher. I have nothing else that I can tell you.'

Sensing that I was wasting my time trying to get more from him, I turned to leave, pulling Baker and Schneider along with me. 'Let's go, boys.' Their weapons had never made it out of their holsters, but they still had their hands on them as they backed toward the door, never taking their eyes from the danger in the room.

Back outside in the passage, with the door guard still watching us, I picked a direction to walk. Mr Perez had been singularly unhelpful again, not that I had expected much, but I had no direction now, no idea which way to go or who to speak with. Looking back at the last two days; I had achieved nothing. I hadn't uncovered a single clue and had spent most of my time pursuing a pair of men that had nothing to do with the missing Cari Gonzalez. Baker and Schneider were trailing along behind me as I drifted along the passage lost in my own thoughts. When we reached an intersection that provided a choice of new directions, I realised that I didn't know where I was, but that minor detail was insignificant when I compared it to the fact that Baker and Schneider were now both face down on the floor and twitching. They had been tasered by two men that I didn't recognise.

A third man appeared between the two men I could already see. He was using his phone, his thumbs a blur as he typed a message to someone. 'Won't be a moment,' he said without looking up, his politeness causing me to wait patiently, even as my two voluntary bodyguards twitched by my feet.

The man was in his forties and slim like an athlete. His head and face were shaved clean, and I could see that his hairline was receding. Like Mr Perez's bodyguards, he was wearing a dark suit and shiny black shoes. The suit looked hand-cut and fit his body precisely. I recognised him instantly from the picture Jermaine had found: it was Kasper Nowak. In contrast to Kasper, his bodyguards were tattooed and dressed in sportswear. The tattoos started at their fingers and though I could only see their wrists, hands, necks and faces, most of the available skin was inked. They were still pulling the triggers on their taser guns, but neither man was looking at their victim; they were looking at me.

One spoke from the side of his mouth, the question aimed at his boss, 'Is dis da one, boss?'

The man's phone made a whooshing sound as he finished his message and sent it and he finally looked up. 'Mrs Fisher?' he asked, his accent distinctly eastern European but somehow also not as if it had been tainted by living somewhere else for too long.

I nodded rather than speak. 'That's enough now,' he said as he stepped forward. The comment was aimed at his thugs, both of them somewhat reluctantly releasing their triggers to finally stop pumping volts through Baker and Schneider. As they began to retrieve the taser wire, Kasper Nowak stepped between them and extended his hand. 'Good morning, Mrs Fisher.' Automatically, I shook hands, wondering how he knew who I was. 'So pleased to finally meet you. I told Viktor the lady he grabbed earlier couldn't be the woman I was after.'

'You have Lady Mary?' I asked. Whoever they were, I had inadvertently found the men that had taken her.

'Lady Mary?' he echoed. 'No, I don't think so. She said her name was Barbie.' My heart stopped for a second.

'Why have you got Barbie?' I asked, my voice barely a whisper.

'I'm afraid we didn't have a description to go on. Just that the woman we needed was staying in the Windsor Suite.' So that was why Lady Mary had been taken; whoever had her had seen her leaving my suite and grabbed her thinking she was me. The same thing had probably happened to Barbie when she left. 'Of course,' Kasper added, 'he could have just said the woman we want is the worst dressed person on the ship and I would have found you immediately. I'm not a fashion critic, but what is with your ensemble? Is it laundry day?'

I glanced at my outfit, the items I had found to fit me from Lady Mary's wardrobe did clash a bit, but I hardly felt they required such harsh assessment. A rather more pressing agenda item occurred though. 'Why do you want the lady staying in the Windsor Suite?' I asked, but I wasn't sure I wanted to hear the answer.

'Should we get out of sight, boss?' the tattooed thug to his left asked.

He nodded, looking about to take in the two motionless, white-uniformed security guards on the deck. 'Probably for the best,' he said which apparently was code for grab the lady and take her somewhere against her will. I considered screaming for help, but I wanted to know where they had Barbie stashed, so I let them pull me down a passage on our left. Before I had to repeat my question, Kasper started talking again.

'One of Eduardo's personal security was kind enough to tell us that you were a friend of Miss Gonzalez and would be able to lead us to her. He said you were a detective of some kind and that you were working for that backstabbing pig Perez.'

'Yeah,' chipped in one of his thugs, 'but Ziggy here silenced him before we could get your description.' The other thug, the one I now knew to be called Ziggy, managed to look embarrassed.

'He was about to grab my gun,' he protested.

Kasper said, 'He was losing consciousness from blood loss because you stabbed him too many times, Ziggy, and he collapsed forward toward your gun. How many times have I told you to aim for the fleshy bits?' They were arguing back and forth like they were talking about what food to order for dinner, not a man's life. Then Kasper turned his questions back to me. 'How about you just tell us where Cari Gonzalez is? Then maybe we can avoid all the unpleasantness, force Eduardo to hand them over and get home.'

'Will you let Barbie go if I do?' I asked, avoiding pointing out that I hadn't a clue where Cari was for fear they might decide they didn't need me if I was of no help or perhaps decide I was lying and do their best to motivate the truth from me. While my mind whirled, I was led through a door and down several flights of stairs. Only once I had been guided through another door and into a new passageway, did I realise that I hadn't managed to take in which deck we were now on.

While I added yet another item onto my list of things to worry about, we arrived at a cabin door, which the nameless thug spoke to in what I thought was Polish. A reply came from inside and the door swung open to reveal a third and fourth tattooed thug, both also wearing sports gear. As they moved out of the way, I could see into the room, where, on the bed, just a few yards across the room, was Barbie, tied up and tied to the bed. She had a scarf tied around her mouth so she couldn't speak and on a couch by the porthole window was a man and woman of about my age, also tied up. They were wearing their pyjamas and looked terrified.

'Gadicia!' exclaimed Barbie as I was bundled through the door. I could see her eyes were puffy again, the shock of her capture no doubt bringing a few tears though there was no other evidence that she had been crying. She was trying to speak through the scarf, but it was muffling her words. I went over to take the scarf off, but Kasper clicked his fingers and Ziggy grabbed my arm again, stopping me before I could get to her.

'Miss Gonzalez,' Kasper reminded me. 'I want to know where she is.'

I was about ready to wet myself with terror but if I admitted I didn't know where Cari was, they would just tie me up like the others. Or kill us all. I was going to have to bluff my way out of this, find help and hope they would surrender. I was thinking fast, the only clue I had latched onto so far was that they seemed to want something from Eduardo; the thing he cryptically refused to identify earlier. I gave it a moment's consideration, then started lying, 'Mr Perez has indicated that he is prepared to hand over what you are after in exchange for Cari Gonzalez.' I wanted to know what the thing was.

'But I do not have Cari Gonzalez, Mrs Fisher. That is why I need you,' he replied sternly giving nothing away. 'Once I have Cari Gonzalez, she will tell me where Eduardo has stashed it and I will get it for myself. She's going to tell me where it is, or I will cut off her other hand.'

'Someone cut off one of her hands!' I blurted, shocked and horrified that the girl I had seen just a couple of days ago was now missing a hand.

'No,' he replied in an exasperated voice. 'I will cut off one of her hands to get her attention,' he added as if it was a perfectly reasonable thing to do. 'Then, if she doesn't tell me what I want to know. I will cut off her *other* hand.' I felt faint. All these men did was cut bits off other people or stab them or shoot up the place. Human life meant nothing to them. 'Now,' he continued, 'I would like you to fetch Miss Gonzalez and bring her to me.' They were letting me go! 'Marcin and Ziggy will accompany you,' he added, shattering my brief excitement. 'I suggest you do not make me wait too long, Mrs Fisher.'

Ziggy grabbed my arm yet again and turned me toward the door. 'Let's go,' he insisted, his tone terse.

'Gadicia?' Barbie said again but all I could do was go with the Polish thug as he hauled me toward the door. I tried to smile at her, hoping I could impart that I had a plan. I didn't have a plan though; I was in trouble and my friends were in trouble and I was at the centre of it.

Just before the door shut, Kasper Nowak had a final bit of advice for me. 'Don't make any trouble for my men, Mrs Fisher. If you attract attention to yourself, they will kill you first and when I hear of it... well, let's just say Herr and Frau Kranz and your rather attractive friend here,' he indicated Barbie as he played with a strand of her hair, 'will never be seen again.'

I was still staring open-mouthed at him when the door was shut in my face and Ziggy tugged my arm again. 'Which way?' he demanded. When I didn't answer immediately, he gave my arm a painful squeeze.

'I am just orientating myself,' I snapped. Despite the threats from Kasper, I couldn't envisage any solution where anyone got out of this alive without the involvement of the ship's security team. I was going to have to lead Ziggy and Marcin on a wild-goose chase until I found some white uniforms and could escape.

I spun around to face down the passageway, genuinely trying to orientate myself, gave up and picked a direction. I found that below deck eighteen, above which were the decks containing the suites, all the passageways in the accommodation decks looked the same; I would have to find a stair or junction with a label to even know which side of the ship I was on. Thankfully, the ship is so vast that going anywhere takes time and I could string the two thugs along without raising suspicion. For a while at least.

Reaching an intersection with a stairwell, I was able to note that I was on deck fifteen and about halfway along the length of the ship. Not that this was particularly helpful since I didn't know where I would find any of the ship's security team. I wanted to head up the stairs; on the upper deck I would be more likely to run into one of the senior officers and be able to signal silently that I needed help I hoped. As I turned toward the stairs to go up, the two thugs, who had until then been conversing in Polish, switched to English. 'Where are you taking us?' Ziggy asked.

'You wouldn't be trying to get us to a public area, would you?' added Marcin.

'I am taking you to Cari Gonzalez,' I replied, lying through my teeth.

'I don't think you are,' replied Marcin. 'I don't think you know where Cari Gonzalez is.'

'Why would you think that?' I asked, trying to bluff my way out.

I didn't get to hear why though because someone shot him.

Marcin's mouth had been open to answer my question when his head snapped back. As it came forward again, there was a neat hole just left to the centre of his forehead. He looked confused briefly, then sank to his knees and keeled over.

Ziggy stared down at him, shocked. Then looked at me but I heard a second puffing noise, one I had ignored a few seconds ago when I first heard it, and he too collapsed to the deck.

As my face wrestled with which emotion to go with, I willed my feet to move. Would I even hear the third puffing noise before I got mine? Rooted to the spot, I jumped out of my skin as a deep booming laugh cut through the silence of the stairwell behind me.

'I knew they would stick to the stairs,' said the voice with a thick accent. 'Boris is always right.' Then he switched to a different language, one I thought might be Russian. He was still behind me, coming down from the next landing. Slowly, I turned to find a pleasant looking man in his late fifties. He had a nice smile, a full head of sandy blonde hair plus a tanned face and a wide smile filled with perfect white teeth which he flashed at me. He wore a pair of tan shorts, deck shoes and a short-sleeved light blue shirt; he looked like he could be a dentist on vacation, and he was talking into a small hand-held radio; speaking to someone else though I could not understand what he was saying.

He had saved me from Ziggy and Marcin, but the handgun fitted with a silencer did not fill me with hope that I was now in good company. Reaching the bottom of the stairs, he let go of the button on his radio and flashed me the smile again. 'I knew they would stick to the stairs. The lazy guests all use the elevators, which means the stairs are almost always devoid of people.' He waved off a compliment I wasn't about to give him and said, 'This isn't my first cruise and Boris knows people.' He laughed again, tickled by something. Then he noticed my clothes. 'Goodness, woman, what are you wearing?'

I didn't answer. Mostly because fear had stolen all the moisture from my mouth, but also because my wardrobe choices were not worth explaining and the theme of critique they were drawing was getting boring.

Perhaps sensing my terror, the man said, 'Please, forgive me, I failed to introduce myself...'

'You're Boris the Russian,' I supplied, my brain finally getting into gear.

He nodded, acknowledging what I had said. 'You are working for Eduardo, Mrs Fisher. That is a mistake.' I felt like countering his claim, but it seemed pointless. 'He has proven that he is not to be trusted. I thought him to be a close, personal friend, which is why I will kill him myself; letting someone else do it would be impolite. I sense that you are not to be underestimated though, so I won't do so.' Above us I heard a door open and more voices speaking Russian – the person at the other end of the radio no doubt and whoever else was with him. 'I wish to broker a deal, Mrs Fisher,' said Boris.

I said, 'Huh?' since I had no idea what he was talking about.

'I want the shoes, Mrs Fisher. I assume that everyone else has tried threatening you, a tactic that does not appear to have yielded a result yet. I will not waste my time repeating the mistakes of others, so I propose to broker a deal. There must be something you want in exchange for Cari Gonzalez.'

'Why do you think that I have her?' I asked.

126

'Come now, Mrs Fisher. I have already... convinced,' he chose the word carefully, but I was certain it was a replacement for the word torture, 'one of Kasper's men to talk to me. He was very clear that they didn't have her, and I just overheard you saying that you were taking them to her.'

Dammit. I had as well. He had overheard my lie and I was in ever deeper now. I needed to go back to the thing he had just said though. I had been piecing bits together as I went, trying to make sense of the rival gangs' interest in Cari Gonzalez. It had been starting to make sense, but now I was more confused than ever. He wanted some shoes? I was certain that I hadn't mis-heard him, but if I asked him for clarity, it would show him how ill-informed I am.

Before I could answer him, the approaching voices reached the landing above us and turned the corner so I could now see them. Six men, all wearing bright, gaudy shirts and tan shorts, no doubt so they would blend in with the guests and not look like gangsters. As they reached our level, one spoke to Boris in Russian.

'English, please, Viktor, we have a guest,' Boris chided.

'Sorry, Boris,' Viktor replied. 'Is that Kasper's men?' he asked, pointing to the two bodies lying motionless either side of me.

Glancing down, I saw that a pool of blood from Ziggy's head was about to reach my left shoe. I said, 'Ewwww,' as I shuffled away from it.

'Yes. I found them accompanying Mrs Fisher. It seemed simpler to kill them than to ask them to hand her over. Now, Mrs Fisher,' he continued, his attention back on me, 'perhaps we can discuss the whereabouts of Cari Gonzalez.'

'Two of my friends have been taken,' I said in response. I wanted to control the conversation if I could, asking questions rather than answering

127

them. I would learn nothing if I was the one giving the answers. 'Do you have one of them?'

Boris frowned, but looked about at the men behind him. 'Do we?' he asked them. The men all looked at each other. I would say they looked innocent but that would be stretching things so let's just say that I believe them when they claimed they hadn't taken Lady Mary. 'I guess someone else has them.' Boris concluded.

'One of them, a young lady, is being held by Kasper. I need help to get her back. And the other guests he is holding,' I added quickly, remembering Herr and Frau Kranz.

Boris had an incredulous look on his face when he said, 'I'm not in the rescue business, Mrs Fisher.'

I pursed my lips. 'I thought you wanted to broker a deal. You asked what I want in exchange for Cari Gonzalez. What I want is my friends back.'

I glanced at the floor while he sucked air in through his teeth and tutted. The pool of blood was getting close again. 'Mrs Fisher, I am willing to broker a deal, but I am not inclined to storm wherever Kasper has holed himself up just to rescue someone I have no interest in. I will, however, storm Eduardo's cabin if I have to. I want you to bring Cari Gonzalez to me. I will not harm her or you if she tells me where Eduardo has hidden the shoes.'

'I will need some time,' I said, butterflies fluttering in my stomach as I began once again to hope they were going to let me go.

Boris nodded. 'No, Mrs Fisher, there is no more time. Tell me where Cari Gonzalez is now.' When I failed to respond immediately, he pointed his gun and pulled the trigger. Thankfully, it wasn't pointed at me, but at

Ziggy's back. His corpse twitched and settled again, but I nearly wet myself anyway. 'The next one goes in your leg, Mrs Fisher, the one after that in your other leg. If you wish to continue resisting, I have quite a few bullets.'

'She's in my suite!' I blurted. It was an outright lie of course, but they couldn't know that, and I was praying that its position on the top deck and the crowds they would find there would convince them to stay away.

Boris smiled though. 'Lead on, please, Mrs Fisher. I look forward to concluding this business. I have a family to get back to and business interests that are not being managed while I am here reclaiming what is rightfully mine.'

Barely able to think straight, I was terrified about what they would do after they discovered Cari was not in my suite and I had lied. Despite my brain feeling like it was underwater and struggling for air, I heard his comment about recovering what was rightfully his. So, whatever Eduardo had, maybe the term shoes was code for something, it was something that belonged to Boris. Hold on though, if that's true, why is Kasper here? Or the Caprione brothers for that matter?

Boris made a giddyup noise that was supposed to get me moving and a hand shoved my back, but Viktor leaned in to whisper something in Boris's ear which caused him to raise his hand and stop everyone before we got moving.

A fast and terse discussion between the two men went back and forth for thirty seconds. It was all in Russian, the nature of it unclear until Boris slapped Viktor hard on his right shoulder like he was congratulating him.

He turned to face me as he said, 'A change of plan, Mrs Fisher. Viktor and Andre will accompany you, collect Miss Gonzalez and bring her to me. Viktor feels that so many of us travelling the upper decks would draw too much attention as the ship's security guards are undoubtedly already on high alert.'

Viktor separated himself from the men behind Boris, stepping forward to the brink of my personal space. He was six feet and several inches tall and broad across his shoulders with a crew cut hairstyle that made him look dangerous.

'Let's go,' he said, motioning with his radio that I should move. He was waiting for me to move, so I started walking up the stairs in the same direction I had been heading when Boris shot Marcin and Ziggy. I had been up for an hour and was yet to encounter another guest because it was so early. That would change soon though as hungry cruisers went searching for breakfast and the sunseekers started heading to the various pools and sundecks dotted about the ship.

Could I get to my suite without endangering anyone? What if I bumped into someone I knew, and they wanted to talk to me? What if I ran into some of the ship's security? Would Jermaine have alerted them that I had snuck away? Had they already found Baker and Schneider?

My feet moving on autopilot, I climbed the stairs in mute horror for the myriad different terrible ways this could end. Then, in a corner of my panic addled brain, a plan started to form.

I continued to trudge up the stairs flanked by the menacing Viktor while wishing I had put my watch on before I left the suite. I could have borrowed one of Lady Mary's, but it hadn't occurred to me when I rummaged through her clothing earlier. I had no way of knowing what time it was though I estimated it was coming up on seven so there would be a lot more people around when we got back to the guest areas.

Viktor and Andre had been silent since we set off, walking no more than a pace behind me as we climbed. My legs were getting fatigued though, they had climbed too many stairs already and I had five more decks to go before I got back to the top deck I was heading for.

The first part of my plan felt dangerous and relied on a portion of luck. If I pulled that off, I would then have to beg favour from people that would not feel inclined to help me and if they did help me, I had to hope that I had lined up all the clues correctly and wasn't getting it completely wrong.

As we reached the landing on the sixteenth deck, I paused to rest. 'What are you doing?' Viktor asked.

'My legs are tired,' I replied. 'I'm not young anymore.'

'One minute,' he replied in a terse voice.

'Actually,' I started, 'I need to use a phone...'

'No,' he replied immediately, cutting me off before I could explain.

'I have to call ahead to my suite. If I don't warn my butler that I plan to hand over Miss Gonzalez, you will find two of the ship's security in there waiting for you. They have been guarding her since the first night.' My lie was delivered smoothly, and I could see he bought it. He was reluctant to agree though, grimacing as he tried to make a decision.

He swore in Russian and produced his cell for me to use. The plastic cover had a pink, sparkly unicorn on it.

'What the heck is that?' smirked Andre.

'I have a daughter, okay?' snapped Viktor, his hard gangster image shattered. Andre raised his hands in mock supplication and bit his lip so he wouldn't laugh too loudly. 'Here,' Viktor said, thrusting the phone at me. 'I am listening though. I don't like what you say, and I shoot you.'

I didn't take the phone; it was no use to me. 'I need a ship's phone. I need to call the phone in my suite which I can do by dialling the room number. There are ship's phones near every elevator bank so there should be one just through this door.' I pointed through the doors on the landing that would lead onto deck seventeen. 'We could even ride the elevator up and save our legs,' I suggested. When he opened his mouth to say no, I spoke again, 'I won't try to run away. You would just radio Boris and sooner or later my friends would die. I need to give you Cari Gonzalez.'

He didn't like it. He didn't like that I was forcing him to make decisions that he didn't like. He wanted to believe he was in control but with each little change in direction I coerced him into taking, the less control he felt.

'I have to make the call,' I repeated.

'Okay,' he snapped. 'I will be next to you. Don't try anything or I will start shooting people.'

The people he was referring to, were the ones we could hear on the other side of the landing doors. It was probably after seven now and guests were up and getting about their day. The noise increased exponentially as I pushed open the door. Right in front of me were happy holiday makers, blissfully unaware of the drama playing out so close to them. I wouldn't endanger them by doing anything, but I had to free myself from Viktor and Andre and this was how I was going to do it.

The ship's phone was really for the crew to use but there was no device fitted to it, no code to enter that would prevent me from employing it. My hands were shaking when I lifted the handset; I had no idea if Jermaine would be in the suite to answer it.

Viktor positioned himself within touching distance of me, leaning against the wall next to the ship's phone so he could glower threateningly at me.

I dialled the number for my cabin. It was answered almost immediately at the other end, Jermaine's voice instantly recognisable. 'The Windsor Suite, Jermaine speaking.'

I said, 'Patrick, it's Patricia.' I heard him draw in a thankful breath, but there was confusion mixed in with it: I had used a different name deliberately. 'I am heading back to you now. We are going to turn Miss Gonzalez over, so I need you to send the guards away. Come up with a reason and get rid of them. Do you understand what I am saying?' I couldn't give him clear instruction without Viktor knowing what I was up to, so my message was hidden in the nonsense I was telling him, and the wrong name given deliberately in the hope he would understand my message contained subtext.

Jermaine was no dummy though, he got it straight away. 'I'll be waiting, madam,' he replied. 'Will there be anything else?'

'No, Patrick. I think that will be all. We will be with you shortly.'

I hung up the phone, my hand still shaking. If Viktor suspected me, he showed no sign, but then his lip was curled in a permanent surly expression, so I was finding it hard to tell what he was thinking. Pushing himself off the wall, he shoved me toward the elevator, which had just arrived. Guests were getting off, but in the ebb and flow of the human tide, there were currently no people waiting to get on and I was thankful that I didn't have to trudge up another three flights to the top deck.

As the elevator doors swished shut my heart dropped as I saw my error. We were going to arrive in no more than a couple of minutes. Jermaine wouldn't have enough time to get ready! As my knees went weak with a fresh wave or worry, the steel box began its upward motion and there was nothing I could do but hope.

When the ping came and the car stopped, there were a dozen people waiting outside to get in. They let us out and paid us no mind, thankfully too caught up in their own lives to notice the terror on my face. The door to my suite was to the right, around a corner and along a passageway toward the front of the ship. I led the two men the last two hundred feet of the journey with my heart banging in my chest so hard I thought they might hear it. All the way, I was waiting for someone like Mr Rutherford or the captain to spot me. If they approached, they would see the two men and due to the very nature of my involvement over the last two days, the disappearance of Lady Mary and Barbie, they would assume the men were hostiles and a gun battle would certainly ensue.

No one appeared though. The few guests we did pass paid me no attention, so I reached my door without disaster. Fumbling with my keycard, I dropped it, had to pick it up and finally managed to open the door.

'Patrick,' I called, 'There is no need for alarm, I have two men with me that are going to take Cari away.' Bored or frustrated or just desperate to

134

grab the girl and get going, Viktor shoved by me, knocking me out of his way in his haste to get into the suite and shut the door. Andre followed him, the pair leaving me behind in the lobby area as they strode meaningfully into the living area with their weapons drawn.

Across the room, I could see a pair of stocking-sheathed legs sticking out from an armchair. The chair was set at an angle to the wide screen TV in the room so all one could see upon entering was the legs and the bright red high-heeled shoes they ended in.

'Get up, Cari,' growled Viktor. 'You are coming with us now.'

He reached the back of the chair and rounded it, but his head was very suddenly not in the same position it had been as a long, long leg whipped out from the chair to kick him under his chin. One moment he had been looking down at the chair's occupant, the next his head appeared to flip through one-hundred and eighty degrees as it tried to look behind him. Andre had just enough time to slow his own forward momentum before Jermaine, wearing a wig of straight black hair and a little black dress with a halter neck and cut-out side panels, vaulted over the back of the armchair to strike him in his throat with a straight arm.

In the next two seconds, my quiet, reserved and delicate butler, ripped the gun from Andre's hand, then took his arm and bent it the wrong way. Now in control, he threw the man around in a circle so his head collided with Viktor's just as Viktor managed to recover from the first blow.

With the momentum Jermaine had created, there was a terrible crack as the two skulls smashed against one another and both men fell to the floor. Jermaine allowed his own momentum to carry him around in a circle as he lowered into a crouch, his eyes on the two men and his arms spread wide ready for action.

135

He moved like a cat crossed with a ninja! It was the second time I had seen him demonstrate his martial arts ability and it was no less impressive than the first. I knew he was capable and had the element of surprise but had worried how he would fair against two armed men. I wouldn't worry again.

Seeing that the two men were not moving, Jermaine straightened himself once more, brushed some creases out of his dress and turned toward me. 'Are you alright, madam? You gave me quite a scare.'

'Yes, I'm sorry Jermaine. I didn't want to endanger you. That's why I snuck out and left you behind.' He fixed me with a raised eyebrow, his butler's version of derisive laugh. In response I said, 'I need your help now, if you are willing.'

'Of course, madam,' he replied. 'Should I change?'

I was just starting to move toward the computer on the desk, when his question stopped me. Where on earth had he found ladies clothing his size in such a short period of time? And shoes too! His feet were enormous, so he hadn't borrowed them from a woman. I didn't ask if it was his though, I asked, 'Are you comfortable in it?' To me it sounded like a question that avoided opinion on the subject.

'Well...' he shrugged, and I wondered if we were going to try to finish this with my butler dressed as a woman. Thankfully, he said, 'I used to perform in the cabaret. It was the job I originally came aboard for. Despite my qualifications, there was no open position as a butler, so I took the role I could find until the position I wanted became available. I performed a drag act and still have several outfits. I felt it might give me the surprise element I would need to gain the upper hand against whoever was holding you. I will take it off, if you can spare me a few moments.'

'Of course, Jermaine. What about the men though?' I asked.

'I will restrain them first, madam. Then, once I am suitably attired, you can explain what you need me to do. I would very much like to assist in recovering Lady Mary.'

He didn't know about Barbie! I considered not telling him for fear it would add pressure or make him worry, but he deserved to know. He stiffened when I explained what I had seen, but silently continued gagging and binding Viktor and Andre. When the task was done, he said, 'They'll kill her if we don't take her back, you know.' I nodded my agreement and he said, 'Then I hope you have a good plan, madam.'

I hoped so too.

## Begging for Help

While Jermaine hurried to his adjoining cabin to change his clothing, I thought again about my hastily concocted plan. I wanted to call the captain and have him, rather than Mr Rutherford, lead the ship's security detail on an armed raid to round up the gangsters, shooting them if necessary as they rescued all the people they were holding hostage. We would arrive at port in a few hours and there they could carefully empty the ship of crew and passengers to better scour it until they found Cari Gonzalez.

It sounded like a much safer plan and while all that happened, I could find a good book and hide in the bath. However, with great reluctance, I acknowledged that I couldn't allow my fear to dictate a course of action that was likely to get people, possibly people I knew, killed. The men I had met in the last twenty-four hours; the Caprione brothers, Boris, Kasper, even Eduardo, were all dangerous, nay, ruthless criminals that would kill without thought or reflection. If I alerted the captain now, how many of the ship's immaculate white uniforms would be doused in red within the hour?

No. To save Barbie and Lady Mary, and the Kranzes, and anyone else that might be currently held captive and to get to the bottom of this and avoid further bloodshed, I was going to have to trick them into giving up their quest for Cari.

Picking up the phone handset in my room, I dialled the number for the room Kasper Nowak was in. It rung and rung and then rung off. This would be much harder if he didn't pick up the phone. I tried again with the same result. Frustrated that my plan was failing before I got to square one, I tried again.

This time a tentative voice said, 'Hello?'

It wasn't Kasper Nowak, but one of his men. 'Put Kasper on the line,' I demanded. The voice I used wasn't my own, but a rough version with an accent that probably sounded ridiculous. I wanted to ensure I didn't sound like me.

'Who is this?' the man's voice asked.

I sighed as if bored by his question. 'Mr O'Donnell's personal assistant and I don't speak to idiots with tattoos. Put Kasper on the line or things will go bad for all of you.'

At the other end there were muffled voices like a hand was over the mouthpiece. A few seconds later, I heard a new voice, one that sounded like Kasper Nowak. 'This is Kasper. Who am I talk …'

I cut him off rudely. 'Be quiet and listen. Mr O'Donnell does not have time for your nonsense. He is very disappointed that he had to make this trip in person.'

'Mr O'Donnell is dead,' he pointed out.

'Indeed, that is what he wanted people to think,' I lied. 'I can assure you though that he is very much alive and is on this ship. He cannot speak with you right now because he is meeting with the other parties at this time. One of you will be selected to partner with him in his new… venture,' I chose the word carefully because there were still gaps in what I knew. 'His faked death was a test to see if you idiots could work together to further his business interests but, as expected, you are all too greedy and grasping to be left unmanaged.'

Kasper interrupted me. 'When I find out who this is, I will cut out your kidneys and make you eat them,' he hissed.

As my stomach knotted, I pressed on, hoping my voice wouldn't waver. 'He wishes to meet with you in the deck seventeen entertainment lounge in the Wave Crest Cabaret room. It will be open for you. Bring your men there at nine o'clock plus any hostages you are holding. Mr O'Donnell wants this resolved without drawing the attention of the Cayman Islands special forces.'

'We are going to Cayman Islands?' he asked, confusion in his voice. 'I thought the ship's next stop was Costa Rica?'

'Mr Nowak, I do find it surprising that Mr O'Donnell is better informed than you. The mess you and the other fools on board have made has forced the captain to make an unscheduled stop. Did you really think you could kill people on board a cruise liner without consequence?'

'Well... um,' he stumbled.

'You didn't think at all, Mr Nowak. That is the answer you are looking for.' This was going so well. He was completely buying into my act. Now I just had to get off the phone so I could call Boris using Viktor's radio.

'I want to speak to Mr O'Donnell,' said Kasper, breaking my triumphant train of thought. 'I'm not going anywhere until I speak with him,' he added sounding determined and defiant.

I had worried about this happening. I had a way I might get around it but the potential for failure grew considerably with it. What I said was, 'Mr O'Donnell is not available at this time.'

'I'm not leaving my cabin until I speak with him,' Kasper insisted. I imagined him folding his arms and stamping his foot at the other end. Struggling to find the right thing to say, I found that I didn't have to when Kasper said, 'Don't call back until he is ready to talk.'

The dial tone echoed in my ear, a bitter sound of failure and disappointment. This might be harder than I hoped. Jermaine came back into my suite through the kitchen dressed in a black suit with a white shirt and black tie. The suit was complimented by shiny black brogues and to accessorise it he had a black umbrella hooked over his left elbow and a bowler hat in his right hand. He looked like a Caribbean version of Steed from the Avengers.

He saw me take in his outfit. 'Is this acceptable, madam?' he asked as he checked himself in a mirror. 'I have always wanted to wear this while fighting criminals.'

It was better than the dress at least. 'We have to go,' I replied, pushing away from the desk and standing up.

'Do you not wish to change your clothing, madam?' he asked. He was staring at my ill-matching clothes without saying anything further. Not that he needed to. I wanted to change but the time it would take felt like an indulgence for vanity when people were in danger.

'No,' I replied. 'Come on, we have a favour to ask.'

'A favour?'

## A Favour

'Hah!' said Boswell Brinks. 'You have some nerve.'

'Who is it?' called Ramone's voice from deeper inside the cabin.

'It's that woman that had almost had us shot,' Boswell shouted back over his shoulder while refusing to take his angry eyes from mine. I had already apologised profusely, but it wasn't having much impact. 'She thinks we should help her,' he added.

'Not me,' I corrected him. 'There are innocent people in danger, and *they* need your help.'

'I don't believe a word of it,' he spat as he took a step back and grabbed the door to slam it shut. Jermaine's foot shot forward to arrest the door's motion, causing it to bounce back just as Boswell was moving back into his cabin. He heard it thump against Jermaine's foot, his eyes betraying his surprise that we would invade his room. 'Ramone!' he shouted, his tone demanding immediate response.

Ramone's hulking form rounded the corner, coming into sight from a room tucked just behind a small alcove that formed the entrance corridor.

'If I may beg your indulgence, sir,' Jermaine requested, his voice calm and quiet enough that Ramone's already curling fists and bunched shoulders wondered what they were getting excited about and relaxed. He kept coming toward us, but his expression was more curious than furious. 'My friend is being held captive by some men that are likely to kill her. I believe Mrs Fisher can arrange for her release along with the other people that are in the same situation, but she cannot do it without your help.'

'Surely this is a task for the ship's security?' he said. 'They have weapons and training as I found out last night.' Despite the cutting nature of his words, they did not feel like he was intentionally rubbing my nose in them.

'They cannot help,' I replied. 'Not without getting people killed.'

'I believe Mrs Fisher is correct,' added Jermaine. 'The criminals are likely to react badly to any show of force.'

Before Ramone or Boswell could say anything further, I quickly added, 'I have a plan that might enable us to get them all free without bloodshed, but I will need your help.'

'What do you need us to do?' asked Ramone. Behind him, Boswell looked still to be stewing, but he didn't voice an argument.

I moved forward, Ramone's eyes catching the movement. 'Can we come in?' I asked, my own eyes imploring.

He nodded and went to move back but stopped and held up a finger that looked like a fat sausage. 'I have a question: what's with the outfits?'

There was a second of uncomfortable silence but when I laughed, for the first time so far today, Ramone laughed too and then so did Boswell. Even my stiff as a board Butler cracked a smile. 'I had some wardrobe issues,' I replied. Then, turning to look at Jermaine, I said, 'Jermaine has no such excuse. His outfit is one of choice.'

'I cannot condemn a man for a little flamboyance,' said Ramone with an admiring nod at Jermaine. He stepped out of the way so we could come into their cabin and shut the door. 'Now tell me what is going on, please, Mrs Fisher. You have me all a quiver with curiosity.'

'I really am sorry about what happened to you last night,' I said to Ramone's back as I walked behind him. 'What I am about to tell you will explain how it came about though.'

As we entered the main space of the cabin, Boswell, who was now sitting on an armchair next to a small table said, 'I can't wait to hear this.' His snarky attitude had returned and though I couldn't hold it against him, it wasn't going to help.

I didn't have to say anything though. Ramone did it for me. 'Come now, Bos. Let the lady speak.'

Grumpily he apologised and I began to explain, 'When you saw me fall into the pool yesterday, I was there deliberately, not by accident. I was eavesdropping on you because a friend of mine had already heard you discussing how you would kill someone. I know now that you were plotting out a script, but at the time I had reason to believe that you might have kidnapped a woman and be holding her captive.'

They both looked at me with incredulous expressions. 'Why on earth would you think that?' Boswell asked.

'Because a young woman was kidnapped two nights ago and someone on board has her. The woman in question is the intended bride of a gangster that escaped Miami with several rival gangs hot on his heels. From what I can gather, the recent death of the big boss, a man called Dylan O'Donnell left a power vacuum at the top. Several gangs worked for him or in alliance with him, I'm not sure about the exact nature of the relationships, but I think they were subservient to him like he was the Godfather or something. I think they had operated under a shaky truce for some time because Mr O'Donnell controlled them. With him gone, the alliance began to fall apart and then Eduardo Perez took something that belonged to someone else, and they came here to get it back.'

144

'What did he take?' asked Boswell, his interest thoroughly gripped now.

I shrugged as I said, 'That I don't know. At least, not with any degree of certainty. They, and by they I mean two of the gangs including Eduardo, have referred to the item as shoes.'

'Shoes?' asked Ramone.

I shrugged again. 'I don't know if that is a codeword for something else, like if you had a ton of cocaine, you probably wouldn't refer to it as cocaine if you were speaking in public. Whatever it is, I met with Boris the Russian.' I saw the confused look on their faces and backed up a pace. 'Boris is the head of one of the gangs on board. He stated that the item was rightfully his, but I know Kasper Nowak, one of the other gangsters is after it as well. A third group, the Caprione brothers also want to get hold of Cari Gonzalez so they can use her as leverage against Eduardo.'

'Are you getting this, Ramone?' asked Boswell breathlessly. 'This is solid gold. We need to be writing this down. For goodness sake, someone pass me my notebook and pen,' he implored, pointing to a table behind me. Jermaine got there before I could, so with the notebook in his hand, the small man started jotting hurried notes. 'We never could have come up with something this good. I mean, just think about the setting. I would have played this out in alleyways and warehouses, not on board a luxury cruise ship.' Then he paused, tapped the pen against his chin and looked up to say, 'Hold on. I thought you said she had been kidnapped, but you have just described all the gangs on board, and they are all still looking for her. If they don't have her, who does?'

'Yeah,' agreed Ramone.

'That is the question I have been asking myself,' I replied. 'None of them appear to have her as they are all pestering me to tell them where she is.'

'That's another thing I am not clear on,' said Boswell putting his pen to one side. 'Why do they all think you know where she is? You don't know her, do you?'

It was more statement than question, but I answered it anyway. 'No, I don't know her. I met her very briefly when her party arrived, but she doesn't speak English, so I wasn't able to communicate with her. I believe one or more of the gangs have been able to capture one of Eduardo's men and torture them for information. When the gangsters arrived on a helicopter during dinner two nights ago, I think they came as a single group but have since split into their individual factions and are fighting each other as much as they are trying to get what they came for. Banded together, their numbers would have exceeded Eduardo's and maybe they had planned to storm his cabin or quietly convince him to hand over what he has. I doubt I will ever know the truth of it, but I believe they want Cari because they are convinced Eduardo will hand it over to save her life.' I paused to let Boswell scribble some more.

'Go on, please,' he said without looking up.

'Cari left the restaurant with two guards. One was found dead the next morning, but Cari and the other guard have not been seen since. If the guards were captured, they will have told them about me and pointed the finger in my direction because Mr Perez asked me to investigate on his behalf.'

'Why would he do that?' asked Boswell, starting to take notes again. 'Ooh, are you a retired senior police detective or a private investigator?' The thought clearly excited him, and he had his pen poised for my answer.

'Nothing like that I'm afraid. It's a long story which I will happily tell you later. For now, it is irrelevant. What is relevant is that I foolishly agreed to see what I could do when Eduardo asked because I was worried about the girl, but Cari Gonzalez is still missing, and I don't know who has her. What I do know is that Kasper Nowak has my friend, Barbie, and another of my friends, Lady Mary, is also missing, presumably held by the Caprione brothers since they are the only ones left to eliminate from the equation. They are both in terrible danger as are however many other passengers they are holding captive. We will arrive in Cayman Islands in a few hours, and I fear they will kill them all as they make their bid to escape the authorities that will board us when we get there. I know the captain is trying to prevent anyone else getting hurt...' I trailed off what I was saying, and Jermaine came in close to place a hand on my shoulder in support.

Quietly, and with Ramone holding his hand, Boswell asked, 'What is it you need us for?'

Finding my voice, I said, 'There's a piece I haven't told you yet. Do you have a phone to hand?'

He looked at Ramone in confusion, but rummaged in his trouser pocket saying, 'Yes.' As he produced one.

'Search the internet for Dylan O'Donnell, crime lord,' I instructed and watched as he looked down at his phone and pressed a button. It switched to voice recognition for him to repeat the search requirement.

Ramone leaned in close to his lover as they both stared at the screen, and I watched the blood run from their faces. 'That guy looks kind of like you, babe,' Ramone said. Boswell swiped his finger across the screen to see a few more pictures.

147

'I thought you were Dylan O'Donnell,' I told him. 'That's why I brought the ship's security down on you. After hearing you talking about murder and torture, I was certain you were the one that had Cari.'

He nodded mutely.

'I have no intention of asking you to do anything dangerous, I want to make that clear from the start, but I do need the other gangsters to believe that Mr O'Donnell is on board.'

'I thought you said he was dead?' he pointed out, his eyebrows showing his confusion.

'I did say that, and he is. But I think if they see him, they will believe he faked his own death and has been testing them. One thing I do know, is that Dylan O'Donnell never dealt with any of the other gangs in person. It was always through his lieutenants, which means that they don't know what he sounds like and will not be familiar enough with him to notice that a mole is in a different place, or a small scar might have healed suddenly.'

'I don't know, Bos,' said Ramone. 'This sounds pretty dangerous.'

I raised my hands quickly in defence. 'You won't be in the same room as them. I plan to use a magic trick to make you appear in front of them when in reality you are tucked safely away in a different room.'

'A magic trick?' Ramone and Boswell repeated together.

'Madam, are you planning to use the Wave Crest Cabaret theatre?' Jermaine asked, jumping in as if he had finally seen what I was thinking.

'Yes,' I said, nodding.

He grinned a wide grin. 'I have some friends I can call. I think they might be of enormous assistance.'

Over the course of the next forty minutes, we crammed in a lot of planning, devising and script writing until we believed we had something that might work. Boswell's attitude switched from surly grump to possessed enthusiast as he crafted a script he would read. Jermaine disappeared for fifteen minutes, returning to the cabin flanked by two men and a woman, all carrying various items.

Once he had thanked his friends and sent them away again, Jermaine produced a set of keys from his pocket and jangled them in the air. 'I thought we might need these,' he said.

Of course! it hadn't even occurred to me that the Wave Crest Cabaret Theatre would be locked. The entire plan might have unravelled quickly if my butler wasn't so switched on. I called to get Boswell and Ramone's attention. 'How are you getting on there, chaps? Nearly ready?' I asked.

Boswell was still scribbling, using an A4 pad instead of his notebook. His lips had been moving throughout the process despite no noise coming out, though Ramone, smooshed in tight next to him, had been talking non-stop the whole time, giving advice and suggesting ideas. They both looked up at my question though, 'Um, yes,' said Boswell sounding a little unsure. 'It's a bit rough, but this might be some of the best stuff I have ever written. I can't wait to flesh it out properly later.'

'You need to practice your Irish accent,' Ramone said.

Boswell nodded, 'Good point,' he said, then cleared his throat and tried a few words, 'Blarney. To be sure. Top of the morning to you. Bejessus. How's that?' he asked.

It was terrible. He sounded like a man that had read about an Irish accent in a book and had never actually heard one.

'We'll, um, we'll work on it on the way, shall we?' said Ramone diplomatically. 'We need to get changed first. Won't you excuse us please?' It was clear they were going through to their bedroom to change but before he went Ramone spotted something in the pile of props and bits Jermaine was sorting through, 'Is that what I think it is?' he asked, his expression somewhere between shocked and excited.

'Mrs Fisher said you would need to look the part. I can't think of anything that says deadly, killer gangster more clearly than this,' replied Jermaine from the floor. I couldn't see what they were talking about, but as Ramone got up to take a closer look, Jermaine saw me straining my neck to get a look and held it up for me to see.

'What is that?' I asked.

'A replica anti-tank weapon,' breathed Ramone as he hefted it to a shoulder and squinted down its sighting mechanism. With his giant body, that was over proportioned in every direction to make him look like two men rolled into one, his head the size of a bowling ball and giant ham fists, he looked like he could beat a tank without the weapon. With it on his shoulder, he was the scariest man I could imagine. His paisley flannel pyjamas were ruining the effect, but they were easily changed.

The items begged a question. 'Jermaine where did you find something like that at such short notice?'

Still on the floor, he was sorting through a bag of makeup. 'The theatre crew have all manner of props. I think that was purchased for a series of skits with a war theme. They dress up and do a song and dance, that sort of thing.' His response made sense at least.

'We should get moving,' I said, looking at the clock. 'Jermaine, how far is the Cabaret Theatre from here?'

He stopped what he was doing to consider the question. 'Not far actually. From the elevator around the corner, it is just across the atrium when we get off.' He gathered a large armful of clothing, the makeup and some other items as he stood up.

Seeing what was left and how much Jermaine was holding, Ramone put down his anti-tank weapon and opened a closet to retrieve a large suitcase. 'Let's use this, shall we?' he said as he opened it.

Boswell tucked his pad under his arm as he, too, got to his feet. With that, all four us were standing in the small space of their cabin, each looking at the others as we exchanged silent glances. 'Are we really going to do this?' he asked, a touch of trepidation in his voice.

'I have to,' I replied.

'So do I,' added Jermaine.

'You're sure you won't be putting him in any danger?' Ramone asked, shooting a concerned glance at his lover.

I grimaced a little as I answered as honestly as I could. 'Neither of you will be in the room with the gangsters. You will be in a separate room with the camera that will project your image onto the stage in the Cabaret room. Jermaine used to work in there, so he knows how to operate all the machinery. But can I guarantee I have thought of everything?' I shook my head at them. 'I would be lying if I said there is no danger in this.'

Ramone gritted his teeth, but Boswell said, 'I've faced Hollywood critics. This bunch will be a basket of kittens in comparison. Let's go.'

So, we did just that, the four of us; a Jamaican Steed wannabe, a middle-aged woman wearing someone else's clothes and no knickers, a giant bear of a man with an anti-tank weapon dangling from one hand and a man so small he was barely out of the midget category.

Setting up in the theatre took a further thirty minutes but we were ready, and it was time to enact our plan and see whether they would take the bait. The plan was so ridiculously simple we couldn't possibly mess it up. Boswell was going to pose as Dylan O'Donnell, reclusive gangland overlord and murderous Irish redhead. Ramone was going to act as his henchman, a role that required no makeup at all. The Wave Crest Cabaret Theatre had a lock on the outside and a storm seal that had been fitted, Jermaine said, when a flaw in the design of the ship had been exposed during a tropical storm. The seal meant that it was possible to not only lock the door but clamp it in place so once we had them inside, they would not be able to get out. The hard part was separating them from the hostages so that we could get them out before we closed the door. Boswell and Ramone would provide the distraction using the same projector and illusion equipment the magician had used a few nights ago. Boris, Kasper, Eduardo and Hugo would see them at the front of the theatre, but they would be safely tucked backstage where the changing rooms, props, stage scenery and the technical equipment control room were located.

When we gave the signal, they would also escape, using the back door which could also be sealed.

After showing me how to lock and seal the main doors because he would be backstage making the equipment work, Jermaine had used the makeup to give me a small head wound. It looked like someone had hit me on the head as there was a trickle of blood leaking down from my hair line and he had given one side of my mouth a bruised appearance as if I had been hit. Ramone and Boswell were both wearing suits, dark blue for Ramone, and a black pinstripe for Boswell which had been accessorised with a sheepskin coat and dark sunglasses. He looked the part, but whether he looked like the man the other gangsters were expecting to see I couldn't yet tell.

'Tell me again, who are we calling first, please,' said Boswell.

I had Jermaine's phone in my hand, ready to set our plan in motion. 'The first call is to Hugo Caprione. We need him to find Kasper Nowak. You're okay with what you need to say?' I asked.

He nodded as he checked himself in a mirror. 'I'm all good. Just wanted to check I had the names right. Let's do this.' He said in his Irish accent. It was improving but it was still the weakest part of the plan.

As Ramone and Boswell got themselves into position behind me, I pressed the facetime option and dialled the number on the business card Hugo had given me. It rang only once, then Hugo's weathered face appeared on the screen. 'Mrs Fisher. I was beginning to wonder where you had got to. You were not in your suite this morning.' Then, as if noticing my face, he said, 'Are you hurt, Mrs Fisher?'

I had made sure the screen showed only my face when I answered. 'Hugo,' I started, making sure my voice sounded scared, 'I will not be able to bring you Cari Gonzalez.'

'That is an unsuitable answer, Mrs Fisher. I have your friend here. I don't want to cut her up into pieces, but I will if necessary,' he replied sounding bored.

At that point and right on cue, Boswell snatched the phone from my hand. 'Hugo, this is Dylan O'Donnell,' he snapped.

A beat of silence passed. 'Dylan O'Donnell is dead,' Hugo stuttered. 'I went to the funeral.'

'Do I look dead? His retort was delivered with a near thundering tone. Deliberately leaving a gap for Hugo to fill, but when he started to speak, Boswell immediately shouted him down. 'Do you know why I faked my death? Huh? Do you? No, you have no idea because that is how I wanted it. I wanted to see who among you was capable of elevating themselves above the others in my absence. Who among you would demonstrate the leadership required to control the business empire if I wasn't around?'

Still off-balance by the sudden resurrection of his overlord, Hugo tried to cut in again, 'Wh...'

Once again Boswell took control of the conversation. 'Are you about to ask me why? Do you think you deserve to know?' Again, he left a gap, but this time Hugo was bright enough to not speak. 'Good answer. Of course you don't know, so I'll tell you. I want a partner. The empire I have crafted is becoming too unwieldy for one man to manage. Each of you has risen through the ranks to control your own small empire but this little experiment has shown me that none of you are capable of stepping up to the big leagues. Now, I have some simple instructions for you, Hugo. Can you follow some simple instructions?'

'There's no need to...'

'I'll decide what is necessary,' raged Boswell. 'Can you follow some simple instructions?'

'Yes,' replied Hugo grumpily.

'Good. Maybe I'll let you live after all. Go and find that idiot Kasper Nowak and bring him to the Wave Crest Cabaret Theatre on deck seventeen, the entrance is on the port side of the ship beneath an awning. You will find the door unlocked and me waiting for you. If Kasper has hostages with him, I want you to bring them with you. Unharmed,' he added. 'And that means the woman you are holding hostage too.'

'How...'

'Because I know everything, Hugo. I've been watching you since you came on board. I got here before Eduardo because I am the one that knows what's happening. That's why it's my criminal empire and you are a minnow swimming in it. You have all made enough mess already. It's a wonder the ship hasn't been boarded by anti-terrorist forces. I have a helicopter coming to get you all back to the mainland. There will be no hostages taken and no one else is to be harmed. Am I absolutely clear on that, Hugo?'

'Yes.'

'Yes, Mr O'Donnell,' Boswell insisted.

Reluctantly, Hugo Caprione repeated the words. 'Yes, Mr O'Donnell.'

Boswell said, 'Be at the Wave Crest Cabaret Theatre at nine.' Then disconnected. Silence fell upon the room for a moment, but then Ramone broke into spontaneous applause.

'Bos, that was incredible,' he gushed. 'You have never acted a part so well and I know you were adlibbing half of it. You were magnificent.'

Boswell was white as a sheet. 'I can't believe I just did that,' he squeaked. 'That man was so scary. I had to make it up as I went along because I got so scared I couldn't remember my lines.'

'Well, I think you did brilliantly, sir,' chipped in Jermaine.

So, it was I that brought an end to the celebration. 'I'm afraid we have to do that again now. We need to get Eduardo Perez here.'

Boswell backed up to a wall and leaned against it. A better word might be slumped, and he looked exhausted. 'I'm going to need a minute to calm my nerves. Does anyone have anything to drink? I need a stiff shot of something.'

We didn't have time to waste but I also didn't want to push him, so I picked up the phone Jermaine had liberated from Viktor and found the number for Boris.

He answered almost before it had connected. 'Do you have her?' he asked.

'Boris, this is Mrs Fisher. I am no longer with Viktor. We were attacked by another gang, but I have the shoes.'

'You have the shoes?' he asked, his voice incredulous and excited.

I bit my lip and closed my eyes as I tried to get what I wanted to say straight in my head before I said it. 'I think I have the right shoes. One of Eduardo's bodyguards had them, but he was shot and they fell right next to me, so I grabbed them and ran. I just want this to be over so you can have them if it means you will leave me alone.'

'Tell me where you are, Mrs Fisher,' he demanded.

'First, I want you to describe the shoes to me so that I know I am holding the right ones.' This was the key bit of information I wanted. Why on earth were they all after a pair of shoes?

I heard him clear his throat. 'The shoes are old and worn. The black leather is splitting near the tongue, but they are still serviceable. They are a demi-boot, designed to be worn under spats, which is exactly how Mr Capone wore them back in the day. No one cares that they are Al Capones boots though, not really. What they care about is the bank codes written inside the tongues that give access to Dylan O'Donnell's millions. Now, Mrs Fisher. Are those the shoes that you have?'

158

'Yes,' I replied breathlessly, finally understanding why everyone was after them.

'Good. Now tell me where you are, Mrs Fisher!' he screamed, his voice incandescent with frustrated rage. 'I want what should be mine and I want it now,' he said more calmly, then added, 'No harm will come to you.'

I wasn't sure he was telling me the truth about that. He was going to come to me though, that much I was certain of. He would risk everything to get his hands on the money.

'I'm in the Wave Crest Cabaret Theatre on the seventeenth deck. You can find me there.'

He tutted. 'Mrs Fisher, that sounds like an ambush. If you want this to end, you will need to come to me.'

Before I could answer, or even think how to, a hand touched my shoulder. It was Boswell and he was motioning for me to give him the phone.

'Mrs Fisher,' prompted Boris.

I handed the phone to Boswell, noting that he looked reinvigorated and determined. He touched the screen, and the phone made the familiar noise it always made when it engaged the facetime function. Holding it in front of his face, Boswell said, 'Do you recognise me, Boris?'

There was silence from the other end, but Boswell didn't wait for an answer; he launched into the same speech he had given Hugo Caprione, cutting Boris off whenever he tried to speak and giving him clear instruction on what his next steps were to be. When he hung up, I was certain Boris was feeling bewildered and beaten and was going to come to the Cabaret theatre as instructed.

'Three down, one to go,' said Ramone. 'Are you sure you're up to this?' he asked with a tender voice as he pulled him into a hug.

'Just imagine the reviews, Ramone. When we rewrite the screenplay to include this scene it will be like the script from The Godfather all over again.' He turned his head toward me. 'Did I overhear that they are Al Capone's shoes they are all after?'

I explained about the shoes and the bank codes they contained. 'So, this was all about money?' Jermaine asked though it was a rhetorical question.

Ramone answered anyway. 'It can be a strong motivator,' he pointed out.

Boswell looked at the phone again. 'I guess I had better make the last call. The first of them will be here soon. Are you all set up, Jermaine?'

'Yes, sir, I am. We should run a test before anyone gets here,' Jermaine advised.

'Good thinking,' Boswell acknowledged, still staring at the phone in his hand. Resignedly, he pressed the button and positioned the phone in front of his face, checking over his shoulder to make sure Ramone, the bazooka-totting henchman was behind him. I had to admire how well he was handling the pressure of the task because he was clearly terrified by the men he was talking down to. 'Show time,' he said as the call connected and once again Dylan O'Donnell came to life.

'Viktor? Why are you calling me? I told your boss the shoes are mine, so unless you have something I want more, oh,' Eduardo stopped speaking suddenly. He had clearly answered the phone having seen the name displayed on it and started talking before he paid attention to the face in front of him.

'Yes, Eduardo,' drawled Boswell slowly. 'Rumours of my demise have been greatly overstated.' I almost choked as he paraphrased Mark Twain, something I doubted an annoying Irish gangster would even be able to do. Eduardo must not have noticed it though because he remained silent as Boswell gave him the same story about wanting a partner and being disappointed about how they had all behaved. His demeanour was that of a father berating his unruly children. This time though he had an extra element to discuss, 'Tell me, Eduardo, why did you take the shoes? Did you really think the others would not come after them?'

His tone glum, I heard Eduardo say, 'I want Cari back.'

Boswell sighed and pinched his nose as if despairing. 'Everyone is coming here Eduardo. Everyone is coming here so we can get back to Miami. Bring the shoes and bring your men. Cari will be here waiting for you. But be warned, Eduardo, I grow impatient, so do not delay.' Then he hung up the call and when he was sure the line was dead; he reverted to his usual accent and said several naughty words. 'My apologies Mrs Fisher. Holding my nerve has proven to be harder than I thought it would be.'

'How long have we got?' asked Ramone.

Jermaine checked his pocket watch. 'Probably no more than a few minutes before they start to arrive,' he guessed. 'It depends where they are coming from. Eduardo is almost certainly the nearest, but that's why you called him last.'

'We had better get into position,' I said, my heartrate doing its best to remind me what was at stake.

161

'Show time,' Boswell murmured again as he and Ramone and Jermaine headed backstage. I was alone in the theatre when a few seconds later dry ice began to seep out from a pump on the stage itself. Jermaine wanted to make sure the gangsters wouldn't be able to see the bottom of the glass panel used in the illusion. The mist would cover it.

The plan I had drawn up in my head seemed feasible at the time, but now I could see so many holes in it, so many things that could yet go wrong. Would they even come? Would they make it here without running into each other or the ship's security first? Would they take one look at each other and start shooting when they did get here? Would they just shoot me?

The voice that wanted to call Mr Rutherford and flood the place with armed guards had one last go at talking sense into me, but I didn't listen.

Maybe I should have.

When the door opened and men started coming through it, I panicked instantly. Not because I was once again face to face with gangsters, but because I wasn't. Coming through the door was a cleaning crew. They had on overalls and were pushing a laundry cart, the type the cleaners dump the dirty linen and towels into. I could see it had linen in it now.

I was hiding in an alcove, out of the way, where no one would be able to see me. I was supposed to stay hidden until Boswell could convince the gangster to send the hostages backstage where he planned to dispose of them cleanly. Of course, they were going to bundle them out the back and lock the door and I was going to slip out this door and lock it. My part sounded more dangerous than it was, I only had to go about five feet and pull the door shut behind me. As long as I stayed still, the likelihood of the gangsters seeing me was next to nil.

Boswell was already visible on the stage, flanked by Ramone who had the Bazooka still hanging from one hand as if it were just an oversized handgun. But the cleaning crew coming now were going to ruin the whole thing; the gangsters could be right behind them, and I would have even more hostages to deal with.

Believing I might have only seconds, I jumped out from my hiding space to confront them. 'I'm sorry, chaps,' I said, trying to get in front of them, 'This room is being used for a private...' I trailed off what I was saying as the man pushing the laundry cart smiled a wicked smile at me. It was Maurice and I could see the gun in his hand pointing down into the laundry cart.

'Hello, Mrs Fisher,' said Hugo Caprione jovially as he levelled his weapon at me. My mouth dropped open in shock and my legs went weak. I had already blown my plan. That might be a pointless concern though

163

because Hugo was walking toward me with a determined look on his face. 'I think maybe I will just kill you now, just to be sure. I'm not a fan of loose ends.'

'Put the gun down,' instructed Boswell, speaking loud enough that his voice carried. 'Fire a shot now and there will be twenty armed guards here inside a minute. The hostages will be taken care of shortly, but Mrs Fisher has been instrumental in bringing a successful conclusion to this matter, though she did require to be coerced,' he added.

Hugo looked at the injuries to my face again and lowered his weapon. 'If you say so, Dylan.'

'Good. Now, what's with the laundry cart?'

'Hugo kept going forward toward the stage. I was forgotten it seemed. His brother followed him, but Maurice wouldn't be able to fit the laundry cart between the stalls, so he stayed at the back near to me, staring down with his standard surly look. As he went forward, Hugo said, 'You were adamant that we brought our hostage with us. I didn't think we would get very far with her bound and gagged, so we improvised. Neat, huh?'

Maurice grabbed the bottom of the laundry cart and tipped the whole thing over. Something heavier than linen tumbled out.

It was Lady Mary!

'Mary,' I cried and ran over to see her.

'Watch yourself, missy. She likes to be called Lady Mary. Gets quite feisty when you refuse to do so,' Hugo chuckled. 'I've got to tell you; I'll be glad to see the back of her. She was okay last night when she had a few drinks in her. Heck, she even asked for more when we got her back to the empty cabin we found, but once she was sober; wow, she is mean.'

Lady Mary had a gag around her mouth and both her hands and feet were tied. I lifted the gag away and she called Hugo a word that I was surprised she even knew. 'Sorry, dear,' she said, now focusing on me. 'He really is a most loathsome man. Will you please untie me?'

From the stage Boswell said, 'I believe my instructions were that you bring Kasper and his men with you.'

Sounding cocky still, Hugo said, 'He'll be along shortly. He insisted he had to go looking for two of his men that went missing.'

Ziggy and Marcin, I thought to myself. I wonder what Boris and his men did with the bodies?

Just then Boris walked in, flanked by what remained of his crew. 'What did you do with Viktor and Andre?' he asked, still striding through the room. 'They are two of my best men.'

Boswell's eyes flared briefly. He had no idea who the two men were or what had happened to them! I had never mentioned it. I thought he was going to stutter but he recovered his composure quickly. His timbre was derisory when he replied, 'Best men? If you say so, Boris. They will not be joining us.'

'You killed them?' he asked incredulously.

Boswell leaned forward in his chair. 'No, Boris, you killed them. You and Hugo and Kasper and Eduardo when you started fighting each other. If it weren't for you, they would still be alive.' If he planned to say anything more, it was interrupted by the arrival of Eduardo, his men entering the room first with their weapons drawn. Boris's men instantly raised their weapons and Maurice spun to face them – all of them that is. Eduardo had the most men, though fewer than he came aboard with, but Maurice was a lone henchman just like Ramone. 'Lower your weapons, all

165

of you,' demanded the fake Dylan O'Donnell. 'I didn't come all this way and arrange a way home for you all, just to have you shoot each other now.'

While the men had been talking, I had been untying Lady Mary. The knots were tight though and it had taken all this time to get the ones off her legs. Suddenly free, the two of us crawled on hands and knees to get some distance between us and the armed standoff. From just in front, Lady Mary turned her head to look back at me. 'I know I've said it before, Patricia sweetie, but it is never dull around you.'

I wanted to laugh but I was too terrified to manage it. While we crawled to a corner, above us, and despite the instruction given, no one had lowered their weapons.

From just inside the doorway, Eduardo said, 'They both had my men killed. I want retribution.'

'Well, you can't have it,' Boswell cut in before anyone else could say anything. Then he turned his head to the side and said a single word, 'Ramone.'

The giant man next to him took a step forward and raised the anti-tank weapon to his shoulder. From my position, peeking over the chairs at the very edge of the theatre he looked terrifying. A thousand years ago, he could have been the greatest warrior that ever lived, swinging a sword bigger than anyone else's on the field of battle and winning wars just by turning up.

All eyes had swivelled to him even though their guns were still raised and ready to shoot.

Boswell said, 'I am getting bored gentlemen, lower the weapons, obey my instructions that will see you safely off the ship and back home to

Miami, or I will give Ramone the order to fire and every single one of you will die.'

The stunned silence continued for a few seconds until it was broken by Boris. 'I heard a lot of legends about Dylan O'Donnell. The little man that was the biggest man around. I'm sure my comrades in this room have heard many of the same ones. If only half of them are true, your ability to come back from the dead should be hardly surprising, but tell me; when did your ear grow back?'

On the stage, the colour drained from Boswell's face. Oh, my God, what had we missed? Was the real Dylan O'Donnell missing an ear?

'Yeah,' said Hugo. 'I heard that was why you stopped going out in public. You got into a fight when you were a teenager in Belfast and the kid bit off your ear. A week later his entire family were dead, and the kid was found with no hands and feet. That's how I remember it.'

Now all eyes were turning to look at Boswell and Ramone. 'Look, gentlemen, you can put down your weapons or Ramone can open fire. What's it to be?' he asked. Some of the confident swagger had gone from his voice though.

'Do it,' demanded Hugo. 'Tell him to shoot.'

'I will,' Boswell assured him, but the bluff was up and everyone in the room knew it.

Boris said, 'I don't think so.' And pulled his trigger.

There was just enough time to see Boswell flinch before the bullet hit the glass and the screen shattered. Dylan O'Donnell and his henchman Ramone vanished instantly. I glanced at the door; it was our only hope of escape, but I couldn't see how we had any hope of getting to it. Framed in the light coming from the passageway behind him, Eduardo had his gun in one hand and a pair of old, tatty shoes in the other. With a sneer on his face, he raised his gun and shot Boris, the second shot proving too much for the tension in the room to take. As if it had been a starter's shot to get a race underway, everyone tried to empty their guns as quickly as they could, the room turning into a maelstrom of death as bullets whizzed in every direction. Lady Mary and I hugged each other, and the carpet, and I prayed that when I got hit it would kill me instantly and not leave me suffering.

It seemed to go on for an age but I'm sure that less than five seconds elapsed between Eduardo's first shot and whoever fired the last, the gangsters either running out of bullets or falling down dead. Neither Lady Mary nor I moved, not for another thirty seconds and it was only Jermaine's voice that convinced me to move then.

'Madam!' he cried loudly. 'Madam, where are you?'

I heard a groan and the sound of someone kicking a gun across the carpet. Urgent footsteps were coming my way as I popped my head up. 'Over here,' I called, separating myself from Lady Mary so we could both get to our feet.

Jermaine spotted my raised hand and ran across the room to help me up. He was checking me all over. 'Madam, are you hurt? Are you shot? Lady Mary, did any of the bullets hit you?' He was more flustered than I had seen him before.

'We are both fine, Jermaine,' replied Lady Mary. 'Well, despite being parched, that is. I don't suppose you have a hip flask in that outfit anywhere, do you?'

Ignoring my friend's single-track mind, I asked, 'Are Boswell and Ramone okay?'

'They are unhurt, but Boswell came over quite faint when the ruse came apart. I believe he may be suffering from mild shock. Ramone is with him.' Jermaine took a pace away from me, satisfied that I was unhurt, and he began checking around the room. 'What happened, madam? When the screen was shot, Boswell collapsed and I took my eyes off the camera, then suddenly everyone was shooting.'

'Eduardo started it... wait a minute, he's not here.' We were standing in the middle of a blood bath, broken bodies lying at awkward angles where they had fallen, but Eduardo wasn't among them. 'He must have seen his chance, realised that Dylan O'Donnell wasn't back from the dead after all and escaped with the shoes.'

'What shoes?' asked Lady Mary.

'Whoever has Barbie didn't turn up either,' Jermaine pointed out. 'We still have to find her.'

'What shoes, Patricia?' Lady Mary repeated, confused but curious.

I didn't get to answer though because an inhuman sound interrupted my train of thought. 'Aaaaaarggghh!' Boris was getting to his feet, and he wasn't the only one! Grunting against the pain of his wounds he lifted his handgun, bringing it to bear on the only target in the room: us.

I was frozen in fear, but Jermaine was already moving, darting left to draw Boris's eyes away from Lady Mary and me as he became the threat Boris would need to deal with. I jumped as a shot rang out, the bullet missing Jermaine to bury itself in the wood panelling on the other side of the theatre. Then the weapon clicked to empty, the distinct sound of the trigger being pulled on an empty magazine echoing in the silent theatre. Giving it a look of disgust, Boris threw it to one side and faced Jermaine.

Jermaine still had twenty feet to cover which gave Boris enough time to pull a wickedly sharp looking machete from behind his back, raising it threateningly even as Jermaine took his elegant black umbrella from the crook of his left elbow.

What followed was almost magical as I watched my butler pirouette beneath a vicious arc carved by Boris's blade. He popped up as it passed over his head, hooked the handle of his umbrella around the other man's ankle and yanked. Boris flipped upside down, landing on his forehead with terrific force, but Jermaine was already moving onto his next target as across the room two more men, both Eduardo's, also made it to their feet. I could only guess their intentions, but they were both armed and even though their shirts were stained with blood, they had murderous expressions.

Jermaine could not possibly get to them before they shot us, my mental calculation of distance, speed and time causing my breath to catch in my throat. Jermaine, however, wasn't out of tricks. He whipped off his bowler hat and spun it across the room like a frisbee.

My eyes tracked its trajectory, but it contained no sharpened steel brim like that of a James Bond villain, all it did was bump ineffectually against the side of the nearest man's head. It got his attention though, the man turning his head to see where the hat had come from just in time to see the umbrella coming from the same direction. It had been thrown like a javelin, its steel tip hitting the man square in the chest and felling him again. The man beside him looked terrified for half a second, but by then Jermaine had closed the distance and was able to deliver a knockout blow to his chin. Probably regretting that he had bothered to get up, the man slumped to the carpet once more.

The heavy clump of boots on the deck outside, accompanied by raised voices, was soon followed by a stream of the ship's security storming the room and fanning out with their weapons drawn as they looked for danger.

Frozen by their stares the three of us in the Wave Crest Cabaret Theatre stood still and silent until Lady Mary said, 'Anyone got anything to drink?'

I would have laughed but a strip light that had been damaged by a bullet chose that moment to fall from its anchor point. A guard screamed like a ten-year-old girl and shot a hole in the ceiling, and I almost wet myself for the tenth time today.

'Mrs Fisher, Lady Mary, good morning,' said a calm and familiar voice as the captain strode into the room. He nodded curtly in our direction then started issuing orders to his men who scurried about checking for vital signs and making weapons safe.

I rushed across the room to speak with him as the ship's security started carrying out his orders, 'Captain, Mr Perez is still at large as is a man called Kasper Nowak who has at least two passengers and Barbara Berkeley, a member of the crew, as hostage.'

Ever calm, the captain said, 'Mr Nowak is in custody. Both the passengers in question, Herr and Frau Kranz and Miss Berkeley are safe and unharmed.' I sagged at the news, my legs failing me but Jermaine, as always, was ready with a hand to steady me.

'Madam, shall we sit you down?' he asked.

'No. No, thank you, Jermaine. I want to hear what the captain has to say. How was he caught?' I asked. 'Was Mr Rutherford able to track him down?'

The captain tipped a nod in my direction. 'It says a lot about you, Mrs Fisher, that you are still trying to help the man though you have witnessed at first hand, his inability to conduct an investigation and keep the passengers and crew of this ship safe. It is my fault, of course, he simply wasn't ready for the role. To answer your question though; when I took over the investigation, I asked myself what I would do if I had snuck aboard a ship like this and had kidnapped a girl and needed somewhere to hide out. I wouldn't have a room and wouldn't have access to the areas where I might be able to hide. I surmised that they would most likely have forced entry into an empty cabin, of which there are few and were easily searched, or into an occupied room where I could take the guests inside hostage for leverage if I needed it. I had the staff ask guests if anyone had noticed anyone missing since we left Miami. Very few people fail to make friends with other people while they are on board so it was mere hours before I heard a report that a nice Austrian couple had failed to show up for dinner with their new friends as arranged and refused to open the door even though voices could be heard inside.'

'Then it's over,' I said, feeling thankful that none of my friends had been physically harmed.

'Where is Miss Berkeley now, sir?' asked Jermaine, concerned for his friend.

'I'm here,' she said. She had come to find us. Undoubtedly hearing about the shootout which would have been heard in many parts of the ship, she would have guessed it was where we would be. 'Are you all okay?' she asked as Jermaine picked her up and hugged her. I got in on the hug as well, wrapping my arms around both of them even as my butler held my gym instructor off the floor.

I was so relieved.

'I should be getting back to George,' announced Lady Mary as the captain excused himself to deal with the carnage.

'Yes, yes, of course, Mary, I'll come with you,' I replied as I wiped away a tear of happiness. 'He was worried sick.'

'Oh, sweetie, George will be fine. He's a natural worrier. I'm not really going to see him, though he will of course be there. I'm going back to my suite because there are no bars open at this time of the morning and I have a rule that I must drink gin within half an hour of nearly being shot.'

'How many times have you nearly been shot?' I asked.

'It's a new rule,' she grinned.

'Well, I have to second it.' A stiff glass of something sounded like exactly what I needed.

'Me too,' said Barbie. 'I don't plan to do much work today.'

Just then, Ramone appeared on the stage, the guards reacting to the huge man in a suit by drawing their sidearms. The captain roared a command for them to cease before anyone decided to shoot first and ask questions later. We had made him look like a gangster, so their response was not much of a surprise. Boswell, oblivious to the brief panic that went through the room, pushed in front of Ramone to jump down from the front of the stage. 'This is solid gold,' he said, not for the first time. 'Ramone, we have to get back to our cabin and commit this to the computer. We can email it ahead and have them queuing up to meet us when we arrive in tinsel town.'

'These men worked with you?' the captain asked me, surprise in his voice.

'They most certainly did,' I replied. 'Their talent was instrumental in our success.'

The captain pursed his lips as he thought about that but there seemed to be nothing else that needed to be said. Ramone waved goodbye as he followed Boswell from the room, they looked set to lock themselves in the cabin until they won the Oscar for best screenplay. Maybe they would do just that. Jermaine, Barbie, and Lady Mary were all looking at me expectantly as if I was in charge of our motley crew. There was nothing to keep us where we were and the gin bottle was undoubtedly calling Lady Mary's name, so edging around the bodies and trying to avoid getting in the way of the guards, the four of us made our way to the exit.

'Mrs Fisher,' called the captain, getting my attention. 'I shall have to ask you a few questions about what went on here later. I'll arrange to come by your cabin.'

I said, 'Very good, Captain Huntley.' He nodded in salute as we left.

Making our way to the nearest bank of elevators, my frazzled brain was trying to tell me that I was missing something. Eduardo was still on the loose, that must be it, I thought.

Then Barbie said, 'So, who did have Cari Gonzalez?'

As the sun began setting to the west, the orange light dancing on the wave tips, I sat and waited. Next to me, on my right, Mr Ikari, the new deputy captain was silently contemplating something. I couldn't tell what he was thinking but he had a faraway yet focused look to his face and I left him to his thoughts. To my left, Barbie looked to be doing much the same. I had asked if she wanted to join me because I hoped it would help to give her some form of closure on the scary experiences of the last twenty-four hours and Jermaine was standing behind her, there to protect me, but very much also there to support his friend.

Filling in the final pieces might have been impossible if Eduardo Perez hadn't been found hiding out in a lifeboat. Of all the criminals that came aboard three days ago, he wasn't the only one left alive, but he was the only one still standing. When I left the Wave Crest Cabaret Theatre to return to my suite for a well-earned rest, I saw a contingent of the ship's security guards running down a passageway toward me. Jermaine and I had to duck out of their way, but curious as always, I followed them. It transpired that a confused Chinese family had seen a man climbing under the canopy over the lifeboat and had then scared a few people as they started shouting. They thought the ship must be sinking and might have spread panic if there were more people aboard that understood what they were saying.

Reacting to the report, Mr Ikari, in his promoted role for about five minutes at that point, led a squad of guards to inspect the lifeboats. The Chinese family could not now identify which lifeboat it had been; there were so many of them. The mum and dad even appeared to be arguing about which side of the ship they had been on. Regardless, Mr Ikari began carefully searching the lifeboats. Rightfully concerned that the person inside might be armed and thus dangerous, the guards were being very careful about lifting the canopy atop each lifeboat in case a bullet came back out.

The search came to an end, not when they discovered a man hiding in the bowels of one of the lifeboats, but when one of the lifeboats sneezed as they approached it. The new deputy captain issued a command that the person inside identify themselves. But when no answer came back it led to a comedy scene where Mr Ikari loudly instructed his men to release the boat from its mooring.

As the hydraulics started up, Mr Ikari shouted, 'The boat will be suspended one hundred feet in the air and twenty feet from the side of the boat until we reach port unless you surrender now,'

'Don't shoot,' begged a voice from within. The canopy of the lifeboat moved slightly as someone moved beneath it, then an old, black shoe plopped out, bouncing once to land at Mr Ikari's feet. Someone in the crowd of onlookers, security had been unable to keep back, laughed and a ripple of guffaws went through the crowd as a second shoe landed alongside the first one. Mr Ikari couldn't keep the smile from his face, his shoulders shaking slightly as he tried to control his mirth.

'Don't shoot,' Eduardo repeated as a hand and then his face appeared from under the edge of the canopy. I found myself feeling just a little sorry for him as the security guards watched, their weapons trained on him still as he clambered over the edge, lost his grip and fell out, his right foot getting caught in the rope that held the canopy in place so he ended up mostly on the deck but suspended from one foot and looking like an idiot.

The crowd were having a great time laughing at the clown, a fresh round of laughter coming as he tried to perform an ab-crunch to get his hands back up to free his foot. Alas, he was in no shape to perform such a move, necessitating that Mr Ikari finally end the show and send two men to extract him.

In cuffs, he was taken away and the show was over, the crowd no doubt discussing who the man was and what it was that he had been doing in the lifeboat. Mr Ikari collected the boots, but assuming he would have no idea of their significance, I forced my way through the crowd and introduced myself, needlessly it turned out as he knew exactly who I was. I saw him looking curiously at my outfit, thankful that decorum dictated he not ask me about it.

After a short conversation, he stared at the boots in a very different way - with mostly disbelief on his face. Despite my fanciful tale, he summoned a guard to bring him a plastic bag they could use as a receptacle for evidence.

That was this morning, not long after Barbie asked the question about Cari Gonzalez. For three days I had been trying to piece together different clues to work out who had her. The sneeze had given me the nudge I needed to make the parts fit. Though I was fatigued from the adrenalin that had been coursing through me, and I was hungry because I had been up for hours and not eaten yet, it still wasn't time to relax. Instead of returning to my suite to lie down, I had to confirm what I believed to be true against a dwindling timespan; when we docked it would be too late.

'Where to next, madam?' Jermaine asked as I set off.

'To the gym, dear fellow, to the gym.' He frowned at my response, wondering why on earth I thought a workout was a good idea at this time, but he dutifully refrained from questioning me.

Pushing open the door to the gym, I noted that it was the first time I had ever stood in the reception and not seen Barbie somewhere in sight. I knew that she wasn't there of course. After her night in captivity, where she assured me no real harm had befallen her, she had elected to partake in another gin drinking lesson with Lady Mary. She had been awake the whole night worrying that the rough men she was keeping company with might have unpleasant intentions for the pretty blonde girl. Thankfully, they didn't, but now she was free and intended to do nothing but sleep for the next few hours. The gin was to dampen her senses so she could.

The young man manning the reception desk looked up from the computer terminal to flash me a professional smile, which cracked slightly when he took in my outfit but returned just as quickly when he caught himself. 'Good morning. Is there something I can help you with, madam? You're one of Barbie's clients, are you not? I'm afraid she is not here today, but I am sure one of the other instructors can assist you.'

'Good morning,' I replied. 'It's not Barbie I want, actually. I was hoping I might talk to you.' His right eyebrow lifted in question. 'It's Hernando, isn't it?' I asked though I was reading the name from his badge.

'Um, yes?' he asked as if not sure he should admit his name without knowing why I was asking.

I didn't respond right away. Instead, I crossed the room to where a board displayed the staff in eight by ten photographs. Their smiling faces looked back at me. Barbie was there amongst the others and so was Hernando, his full name displayed beneath his picture. I nodded and smiled to myself, then said, 'Thank you,' to his bewildered face and pushed the gym door open once again as I left.

I contemplated confirming my assumptions by myself before telling anyone else, but I was fairly certain I had it all worked out correctly so when I got back to the suite, I asked Jermaine to perform a task for me and called Mr Ikari myself.

'Mr Ikari,' I said when his voice came on the line. 'I believe I have something you may be interested in.' Curious enough to listen, I explained what I knew and what I was guessing and invited him to join me later when I promised to provide a neat ending to the events of the last few days. He asked me where just as Jermaine passed me a note with a number on it – the one piece of information I didn't have and that was how we now came to be sitting on a bench outside the crew exit.

The ship had docked a little more than an hour ago, coming into the Cayman Islands despite the gangster threat being eliminated because the captain had already announced the unscheduled stop and we were almost there when the gun fight on deck seventeen took place. For fifteen minutes we had waited patiently for something to happen, something I had cryptically not explained to the people with me as I begged their indulgence instead. The fifteen minutes was starting to feel like a long time, but just when an early tendril of doubt crept into my head, I heard the sound I was waiting for: paws on the steel deck.

A smile forced its way onto my face, lifting the corners of my mouth as a soupcon of tension I hadn't noticed, flitted away. Muffie was coming our way.

'Is that a dog I hear?' asked Mr Ikari sitting forward. As of some point early today, when the captain had demoted Mr Rutherford and replaced his number two, Mr Ikari had taken on responsibility for the ship's crew, discipline, security and probably many other tasks I wasn't aware of. The crew were not allowed pets, so his surprise that he could hear a dog coming out of the crew quarters came as no surprise to me.

His question caused Barbie and Jermaine to lean forward, their eyes drawn to the doorway the sound was coming from. Moments later, the little dog appeared, held in check at the end of a sparkly lead and straining to get somewhere as dogs do. The dog paid us no mind, but the face that rounded the corner holding the lead took one look at us and skidded to a startled halt.

I smiled at him and said, 'Hello, Hernando Gonzalez.'

As his feet had faltered, the people coming along the passageway behind him had bumped into his back. The question that echoed out, in Spanish I couldn't understand, came from the lips of Cari Gonzalez, her face also framed in the doorway.

'Barbie, gentlemen, this is Cari Gonzalez,' I explained.

Mr Ikari got to his feet, his arms folded across his chest and his face stern. 'This is the woman my men have been tearing the ship apart trying to find for the last three days?'

'And her brother and Enrique Garcia, the bodyguard that went missing on the first night.' With introductions made and the three of them still looking startled, I suggested we all go back inside for a chat. I told you earlier that the sneeze gave it away so let me explain; Barbie, allergic to dogs had been reacting to the presence of one for the last few days, ever since Cari Gonzalez came aboard with hers in fact. Dogs were not common on board the Aurelia, so Barbie had no reason to take drugs to combat her allergy. Equally, she hadn't come into contact with or even seen Cari's little dog, Muffie, so she hadn't realised what was causing her nose to itch. At first, I had assumed she was having boyfriend or relationship troubles and that her eyes were puffy from crying, but having dismissed that notion, my next guess was an allergy and the idea had simmered quietly inside my head until Eduardo sneezed, and I connected the dots. But if she hadn't come into contact with the dog, how was it that she was reacting to it? The answer was transference.

Hernando Gonzalez had known his sister was coming on board. When she was questioned later, it transpired that she had convinced Eduardo to

180

steal the shoes from the allied gangsters and escape to the ship. Her plan had always been to escape but when the helicopter brought the other gangsters to the ship, she had to escalate the timescale of her plan and abandon the shoes and the fortune they might lead to.

Her lover, the bodyguard I knew as Enrique and one I assumed all along to have died on the first night, had shot the other bodyguard and dumped him in a laundry chute, allowing the two of them to escape to her brother's cabin in the crew area where they had been squirreled away for three days. Fearing exposure, they had stayed there, locked inside, necessitating her brother walk her dog. Inevitably picking the dog up, its fur had transferred to his clothing and then, in close proximity to Barbie each day, the hair had transferred to her.

They were caught, but now that I had solved the whereabouts of the kidnapped bride, I got to hear her story and could not condemn her for her actions. She had been lured away from her family at fifteen, offered wages for working in a club as an exotic dancer that she would not have been able to resist. Her family were on the breadline, barely scraping by so she had been able to improve the life of her parents and her younger brother who subsequently went to college before taking a job as a physical training instructor on the Aurelia. Her looks had attracted Eduardo, which had then brought a new, even better, level of lifestyle, but even though she was sleeping with Eduardo Perez, she had fallen for one of the younger men she saw every day and the two of them hatched a plot to change their future.

What would happen to them was not for me to decide though I hoped leniency would follow for Enrique.

Through Mr Ikari, I asked Cari what it was that she had said to me in the ladies' toilet three night ago. The answer she gave was, 'Best laid plans.' She had been laughing at herself because her plan to escape on the ship had taken weeks to plan, the idea forming a year ago when her brother took the job. She had tried to escape Eduardo in the past, each attempt resulting in an even worse beating than the one before, so her new plan was to steal the shoes for herself and escape with Enrique on the ship. Eduardo caught her though as she tried to leave, his jaw dropping at what she had done. Certain the other gangsters would kill her no matter if he returned the shoes, he decided to run. His businesses were failing, he was the weakest member of the alliance, and he knew it, but with sole access to the hidden fortune of Dylan O'Donnell, he could set up somewhere new. Suddenly he had opportunity. He really did set fire to his club to throw the others off his track but was too dumb to cover up the credit card transaction to book his suite on the ship, so they found him easily enough.

When I first saw them arrive at the Aurelia's entrance, Cari was being dragged on board against her will, wondering how she was now going to escape. From there on she had improvised, leaving the note for Eduardo that he had been showing off as a ransom note: I warned you. It was her message to him, but I wasn't sure he had even understood it.

Listening to her tearful story, with her brother and lover being held in different rooms, I could feel nothing but sorrow. A tear leaked from my eye, treacherously running down my cheek as I refused to brush it away. When she finally fell silent, Mr Ikari said, 'Can I have a word outside, Mrs Fisher?'

Surprised, I nodded and followed him into the passageway. 'What is it, Mr Ikari?'

He rubbed his chin, considering his answer. 'I have to alert the authorities that Enrique Garcia is guilty of murder, and I will have to dismiss Hernando Gonzalez, his actions cannot be forgiven. However,

Miss Gonzalez has committed no crime that I can identify so I have no authority to hold her.'

I wasn't happy to hear that any of them were to be punished, but at least Cari was in the clear. 'There's something else, isn't there?' I asked since it was clear he was still wrestling with something.

'Well,' he started, 'I cannot release Miss Gonzalez here, and I probably need to return her to the United States to give evidence against the thugs we have just handed over. I believe I need to check what the official paperwork might say about this matter, me being new to the role and all. I think perhaps I will take my men and go check that paperwork. It will take me a few minutes, of course.'

He stared directly into my eyes to make sure I had understood what he was saying, then called his men and began to walk away from me down the passageway going deeper into the ship. 'Official paperwork, Mrs Fisher. It will take me a while to return.'

My mouth was hanging open and my heart beating in my chest when Jermaine spoke quietly next to my ear and scared the heck out of me, 'I think he just opened the metaphoric cell door, madam. Perhaps we should act quickly.'

The way out of the ship was less than one hundred yards away. I didn't know how long we had but there was no time to lose. *Official paperwork?* Mr Ikari had just become my new hero. He and I were going to get on just fine.

Five minutes later, with her dog clutched under her arm and both her brother and lover running along beside her, Cari Gonzalez escaped to a new life.

And me? I went to find Lady Mary. It was time for a gin and tonic.

The End


Over the page you will find an extract from the next book in this series –
**The Director's Cut** and a link to it if you want to grab your copy now.

## Author's note

I originally published this book in the summer of 2019. At the time, I was in full-time employment in a job that I loathed and looking for a way out.

I had no idea Patricia Fisher would come to my rescue. By the time the sixth book hit the Amazon marketplaces around the world, I was a free man.

Now two years on, I have written over sixty books and regularly find myself atop the cozy mystery charts. Patricia led to other characters who then led to even more characters, and I found ways to interlink them all to create a glorious universe of cozy mystery.

I think you will enjoy them all and each book and indeed all my series, though markedly different from one another, all carry the same fast-paced humorous theme.

There is a full list below along with links to get you free stories and more information.

Take care.

Steve Higgs

## A FREE Rex and Albert Story

There is no catch. There is no cost. You won't even be asked for an email address. I have a FREE Rex and Albert short story for you to read simply because I think it is fun and you deserve a cherry on top. If you have not yet already indulged, please click the picture below and read the fun short story about Rex and Albert, a ring, and a Hellcat.

When a former police dog knows the cat is guilty, what must he do to prove his case to the human he lives with?

His human is missing a ring. The dog knows the cat is guilty. Is the cat smarter than the pair of them?

A home invader. A thief. A cat. Is that one being or three? The dog knows but can he make his human listen?

There is no catch. There is no cost. You won't even be asked for an email address. I have a FREE Amber and Buster short story for you to read simply because I think it is fun and you deserve a cherry on top. If you have not yet already indulged, please click the picture above and read the fun short story about a dog who wants to be a superhero, and the cat who knows the dog is an idiot.

**Marriage? It can be absolute murder.**

Wedding planner for the rich and famous, Felicity Philips is aiming to land the biggest gig of her life – the next royal wedding. But there are a few obstacles in her way ...

... not least of which is a dead body the police believe she is responsible for murdering.

Out of custody, but under suspicion, her rivals are lining up to ruin her name. With so much on the line, she needs to prove it wasn't her and fast. But that means finding out who the real killer is …

… without said killer finding out what she is up to.

With Buster the bulldog as her protector and Amber the ragdoll cat providing sartorial wit – mostly aimed at the dog - Felicity is turning sleuth.

What does a wedding planner know about solving a crime?

Nothing. Absolutely nothing.

Get ready for a wild ride!

## More Books by Steve Higgs

**Blue Moon Investigations**

Paranormal Nonsense

The Phantom of Barker Mill

Amanda Harper Paranormal Detective

The Klowns of Kent

Dead Pirates of Cawsand

In the Doodoo With Voodoo

The Witches of East Malling

Crop Circles, Cows and Crazy Aliens

Whispers in the Rigging

Bloodlust Blonde – a short story

Paws of the Yeti

Under a Blue Moon – A Paranormal Detective Origin Story

Night Work

Lord Hale's Monster

The Herne Bay Howlers

Undead Incorporated

The Ghoul of Christmas Past

The Sandman

Jailhouse Golem

Shadow in the Mine


**Patricia Fisher Cruise Mysteries**

The Missing Sapphire of Zangrabar

The Kidnapped Bride

The Director's Cut

The Couple in Cabin 2124

Doctor Death

Murder on the Dancefloor

Mission for the Maharaja

A Sleuth and her Dachshund in Athens

The Maltese Parrot

No Place Like Home

**Patricia Fisher Mystery Adventures**

What Sam Knew

Solstice Goat

Recipe for Murder

A Banshee and a Bookshop

Diamonds, Dinner Jackets, and Death

Frozen Vengeance

Mug Shot

The Godmother

Murder is an Artform

Wonderful Weddings and Deadly Divorces

Dangerous Creatures

**Patricia Fisher: Ship's Detective**

Patricia Fisher: Ship's Detective

**Albert Smith Culinary Capers**

Pork Pie Pandemonium

Bakewell Tart Bludgeoning

Stilton Slaughter

Bedfordshire Clanger Calamity

Death of a Yorkshire Pudding

Cumberland Sausage Shocker

Arbroath Smokie Slaying

Dundee Cake Dispatch

Lancashire Hotpot Peril

Blackpool Rock Bloodshed

**Felicity Philips Investigates**

To Love and to Perish

Tying the Noose

Aisle Kill Him

**Real of False Gods**

Untethered magic

Unleashed Magic

Early Shift

Damaged but Powerful

Demon Bound

Familiar Territory

The Armour of God

Get sneak peaks, exclusive giveaways, behind the scenes content, and more. Plus, you'll be notified of Fan Pricing events when they occur and get exclusive offers from other authors because all UF writers are automatically friends.

Not only that, but you'll receive an exclusive FREE story staring Otto and Zachary and two free stories from the author's Blue Moon Investigations series.

# Yes, please! Sign me up for lots of FREE stuff and bargains!

Want to follow me and keep up with what I am doing?

Facebook

The whoosh of flame leaping into the air made me jump just as the thump of the explosion that caused it reached my ears. It was so close I could feel the change of air pressure in my lungs.  Across the deck, I watched as Barbie, dressed in a short, figure-hugging red cocktail dress and heels, cowered behind the bar of the upper deck sun terrace. Two bullets gouged holes in the bar next to her head, splinters flying off dangerously as she ducked back again. Her eyes showed the panic she felt.

'Stay there! I'm coming to you,' yelled a man's voice. My eyes swung to see where the voice had come from. Doug Douglas looked handsome in his black dinner suit, but the jacket and trousers had seen better days, ripped as they were on both knees and the sleeve of the jacket hanging open on his right shoulder. There was blood coming from a cut on his left cheek, but he looked more angry than scared.

He was crouching in a doorway that led back into the upper deck accommodation where I knew his suite was located. As he stood up to start across the deck, another explosion threw him across the deck and set fire to his jacket.

Barbie screamed, but stayed where she was, terrified that any movement might expose her to the shooter.

Doug Douglas rolled across the deck, flipped himself upright and with gritted teeth, he ripped the burning jacket from his body and cast it aside. Doing so revealed the twin holsters hung under his arms and as I stared in rapt fascination, he whipped them both out and began sprinting across the deck, guns raised in front of him as he fired shot after shot at a target I couldn't see.

A man dressed all in black, wearing a black balaclava leaped down to the deck from a platform above the terrace, landing neatly on both feet and already shooting at Doug before he was fully standing again. The weapon in his hands was some kind of assault rifle; big and black and lethal looking.

Doug lined up his pair of pistols and shot him, the bullets both hitting him in the chest to bowl him over backward. As the man went down, Doug Douglas leaped over him and fired again as two more men dressed in black emerged from a doorway to his left.

Yet another explosion rocked the ship, knocking him off balance and he fell painfully to the deck as Barbie screamed again. He scrambled to put himself against a low wall filled with plants, part of the decoration of the sun terrace, using the few seconds respite to eject his empty magazines and reload.

I saw him check around, scanning everywhere for danger then get to his feet and instantly start shooting again as five more targets appeared to his front. Bullets hit the deck all around him as he darted forward; it seemed impossible that he could avoid them all but just as I thought that, a puff of red exploded from his right shoulder and he faltered, throwing away his empty guns as he stumbled onward.

'I'm coming, baby!' he shouted above the deafening noise of burning ship.

The black clad men were still coming though. One emerged from a doorway as he passed it; too close for a gun, even if he had one, he grabbed the man's assault rifle, ripping it upward to strike him under the chin, then yanked it downward so the strap around his body pulled him off balance. There was a sickening crunch as he followed him down with an elbow to the back of his head, but he had no time to rest; another terrorist was coming!

This one had a knife which he thrust toward Doug Douglas, only to find Doug was no longer where he had been. Doug whipped a long leg around in an arc to kick the man in his ear, then holding his pose and balancing on one leg, he kicked him in the jaw as his head rebounded, followed the kick through and spun around into a crouch as he scanned for any further danger.

Satisfied that he was safe, for now at least, Doug Douglas stood up, walked across the ruined terrace and offered Barbie his hand to get up. Nervously smiling, she took it and he pulled her into an embrace.

'Doug, you're hurt,' she cried, terror making her voice wobble.

'They're just scratches, babe. Nothing compared with the pain I would feel if I lost you.'

'Oh, Doug,' she swooned.

He kissed her then, amidst the madness and destruction, he folded her back as he leaned into her and stole her breath with his manliness.

As he broke the kiss and brought her back to her feet, a voice rang out from behind him. 'Mr Douglas, did you really think it would be that easy?'

'Doctor Enviro, why don't you stop this madness? Or do I have to stop you?' he sneered.

Doctor Enviro walked into view. He was armed with a powerful looking rifle and wary enough to keep his distance from Doug Douglas. Doug wasn't armed and once again Barbie was looking utterly terrified.

Doctor Enviro laughed. It sounded evil and false, but as its mirth ended, he said, 'I think it is time I taught you a lesson for interfering in my affairs.' Then he pulled the trigger on his giant gun, startling Doug as he moved to protect Barbie. He was too late though. The shot had hit her just below her perfect left breast.

She had time to utter a single word, 'Doug,' as she fell, Doug Douglas catching her before she hit the deck. She looked into his eyes for a moment then, as my heart stopped from the spectacle I was witnessing, her head lolled back.

Behind him, Doctor Enviro cackled.

## The Director's Cut is available by clicking this link

Made in the USA
Las Vegas, NV
04 April 2024

88240511R00121